The Neighborhood Kids

The Neighborhood Kids
Short Stories Reader

Richard L. McBain

READERSMAGNET, LLC

The Neighborhood Kids
Copyright © 2018 by Richard L. McBain

Published in the United States of America
ISBN Paperback: 978-1-947765-39-9
ISBN eBook: 978-1-947765-65-8

All rights reserved. No part of this publication may be reproduced, stored in a retrieval system or transmitted in any way by any means, electronic, mechanical, photocopy, recording or otherwise without the prior permission of the author except as provided by USA copyright law.

The opinions expressed by the author are not necessarily those of ReadersMagnet, LLC.

ReadersMagnet, LLC
10620 Treena Street, Suite 230 | San Diego, California, 92131 USA
1.619. 354. 2576 | www.readersmagnet.com

Book design copyright © 2018 by ReadersMagnet, LLC. All rights reserved.
Cover design by Ericka Walker
Interior design by Shieldon Watson

DEDICATION

This book series is dedicated to my Grandchildren
Nathan, Cade, Mattie, and Carter McBain

CONTENTS

Book Proverb 9
Acknowledgements 11

Story 1   Accidents Happen 13
Story 2   Social Media Nightmare 21
Story 3   The Story Teller 29
Story 4   Always Bigger And Better 37
Story 5   Never Admitted Doing Wrong 43
Story 6   Backed Into A Corner 51
Story 7   They Never Hurt Anyone Until 57
Story 8   Lying To My Parents Is No Big Deal 63

Good Manners Make You The Poster Child For Smart

Story 9   Why Don't People Like Me? 73
Story 10   Chaos At The Family Table 79
Story 11   The Shortsighted Neighbors 85
Story 12   Just What Is The Golden Rule 91
Story 13   Being Polite Earns Respect 99
Story 14   Credibility Comes From
                The Way People See You 103

Story 15	Saying I'm Sorry Helps Considerably	107
Story 16	Gracefully Accepting Bad News	113
List Of Good Manners		119

Cheating Can Make You A Dead End Kid

Book Proverb		129
Story 17	No Big Deal, I'll Just Copy Hers	131
Story 18	A Bike Race With Troubles	137
Story 19	It's Only A Game	143
Story 20	Going For The School Record	149
Story 21	Great Idea, Even If It's Not Mine	155
Story 22	She Will Never Know	163
Story 23	Why Would She Do That To Me	171
Story 24	The Better One Should Be Mine	179

Catch A Wave With Respect & Obedience

Book Proverb		187
Story 25	Playing Favorites Is Not The Way	189
Story 26	A Girl Who Had A Better Way	195
Story 27	They'll Never Find Out	203
Story 28	Come On, She's Just A Babysitter	209
Story 29	The Ocean Must Be Respected	215
Story 30	That's The Last Time	221
Story 31	Oh No, What Am I Going To Do	229
Story 32	I Wish I Had Listened	235
About The Author		243

BOOK PROVERB
(that gives advice about how people should live)

The importance of being truthful,
Is a most wonderful thing you see,
For it is the real
substance,
That gives you
integrity!

Integrity—the quality of being honest and having strong moral principles; moral uprightness. "he is known to be a man (or woman) of integrity"

ACKNOWLEDGEMENTS

Merriam-Webster
Publisher company

Merriam-Webster, Inc., which was originally the G & C Merriam Company of Springfield, Massachusetts, is an American company that publishes reference books, especially dictionaries that are descendants…Wikipedia

Dollar Photo Club
www.dollarphotoclub.com

STORY 1

ACCIDENTS HAPPEN

Whack, went the bat when Bobby hit the ball hard and started to run to first base. Tommy went running back after the ball that just happened to crash through Mrs. Jones window.

Everybody began to run in all directions to get out of sight before Mrs. Jones would come out to see who was responsible for breaking her window.

Tommy was still standing near her window when Mrs. Jones came out with the ball. "Did you break my window?" asked an angry Mrs. Jones as Tommy realized he was the only one in sight of this upset woman.

"No Ma'am", replied Tommy, "we were all playing baseball and a hard hit made the ball hit your window", he said. "Well I want to know who is going to pay for this window?" she said while tossing the ball up and down in her hand. "Who hit the ball?" she asked.

Tommy was stunned at the question. He didn't want to be a snitch on his friend Bobby, but he also knew it was wrong to lie so he wasn't going to do that either. "Mrs. Jones, I can't tell you who hit the ball because I don't want to be called a snitch", he answered truthfully.

Mrs. Jones' voice became angry as she said to him, "well you better tell me or you are going to pay for the window, and I'll call your parents", she quickly said. Tommy didn't know what to do so he simply said he needed time to think about it, and would get back to her soon.

As he walked away she shouted after him that he had better get back to her soon or she would call his parents. Her question presented Tommy with a moral dilemma.

> **MORAL DILEMA**
>
> A *dilemma* ("double proposition") is a problem offering two possibilities, neither of which is good to do.

His choices were to tell on his friend; be labeled a snitch, and have his friend mad at him, or to have to pay for a window that he didn't break. He decided the right thing to do was to talk with his friend Bobby and have him go to Mrs. Jones and tell her he broke her window.

He went to Bobby's house and when Bobby came to the door, Tommy said, "come on outside Bobby, I need to talk to you." Bobby knew what Tommy probably wanted to talk about, but ignored that and started his own conversation.

"Pretty awesome hit I had today", Bobby bragged. "Yeah and it smashed right through Mrs. Jones' window", Tommy interrupted. "It was a great hit Bobby with only one problem", he said, "Mrs. Jones came out and asked me who was going to pay for the window".

"You didn't tell her I did it did you?" he asked. No, but she said if I don't tell her who is responsible she will call my parents and have me pay for it, said Tommy. "All you have to do is tell your parent's that you don't know who did it and that will be the end of it", Bobby replied.

"No, I won't do that", Tommy said, "Because that would be bringing me into the wrongdoing by lying to my parents. You need to go to Mrs. Jones and tell her you did it by accident, and then pay for the window. That's the best way to make this right". Bobby shook his head not liking the suggestion his friend had just made.

"Heck no, I'm not 'gonna do that. She has no idea I was even there, and besides, I don't have any money anyway". Tommy didn't like what Bobby was saying because he was now putting him in a predicament.

(Predicament—a difficult or unpleasant situation)

The boys went back inside Bobby's house and up to his bedroom. "Bobby you are leaving me no choice. I will not lie to my parents, and I will not pay for your mistake. Now she knows that I know who hit the ball and either you tell her you did or I will have to".

Bobby got up from sitting on his bed and walked toward Tommy saying angrily, "I thought we were best friends, and now you're going to snitch on me? I wouldn't do that to you!"

Tommy quickly responded saying, "You wouldn't have to because I would never put my best friend in a place where he would be responsible for my mistake, and I sure would never tell you to lie to anyone. You know Bobby; right is right and wrong is wrong. It's actually stealing from that woman if you expect her or anybody else to pay for what you did, whether it was an accident or not".

With that, Tommy began to walk out of Bobby's room. As he was going out of the door, he turned to Bobby and said, "You only have a short time to make up your mind, so you'd better hurry. You know what's right to do here Bobby, so please don't make me have to do something I don't want to do", he continued, and then left the house.

Bobby lay down on his bed hoping homework he had to do would take his mind off of this problem, but it didn't. He then tried to figure the whole thing out, thinking he had gotten away with breaking the window, but he knew that was wrong. Then he began to think of the predicament he had put his friend in who would either have to pay for the window himself, or snitch on a friend.

Next he thought that if he went and admitted to breaking the window, where would he get the money to pay for it? If he borrowed it from his parents, they would know he tried to ditch the responsibility of what he had done, and if he didn't, it would take weeks of his allowance to pay it off. He didn't think that Mrs. Jones was going to wait that long to have her window fixed, so his parents would find out anyway.

He soon knew he had to make things right, and first found Tommy. He approached him and hung his head. "I'm sorry Tommy, I never thought through this until you explained it that way", he said. "You're my best friend and I would never want you to do things that are wrong. It's one of the things I admire about you so much, as do all of the other guys. You always do what's right, and the good of it is always obvious to all of us. I'm not sure where I'm going to get the money to pay for it though, but I guess I'll ask my Dad", he concluded.

Tommy had been thinking about this situation and had come up with an idea. "Look Bobby, we were all involved in the game, and if all of us chipped in a couple of dollars that should cover it don't you think?" he asked. "Why don't you go over to Mrs. Jones house and tell her it was an accident and you're sorry you ran, but were just scared about doing it. Meanwhile I'll find the other guys and get them to chip in for the window. Make sure you find out from Mrs. Jones how much it will cost", he said.

Bobby was thankful for his friend coming up with a great idea that seemed fair to everyone. He also felt much better because he was going to make things right about this with everyone's help.

Mrs. Jones was pleased that Bobby came and confessed that he had hit the ball, and told him it would come to twenty-two dollars. Since there were nine players, everyone would have to chip in two and a half dollars.

Tommy was able to get to the other guys who were playing the game with them when the window was broken, and they all agreed this was a fair way to take care of the problem.

The boys all chipped in their part and Tommy and Bobby took the money over to Mrs. Jones, again apologizing to her. Mrs. Jones was very pleased that the boys had done the right thing, and all was well once again.

> **MORAL OF THE STORY**
>
> The window was broken, and leaving Tommy to take the heat, was an act of dishonesty. Fortunately Tommy, because of his integrity with the group, was able to convince them all to do the right thing.
>
> Making things right by being honest and accepting responsibility when we do something wrong, whether we meant to or not, will always make us feel better, and build that great and noble trait that people respect—INTEGRITY!

STORY 2

SOCIAL MEDIA NIGHTMARE

Meghan and Susan were neighbors and had been close friends for ten years. As they entered their twelfth year, they both received smart phones from their parents for Christmas. The first thing they both did was get together to explore the different things they could do with the phones. They downloaded the app (application) to a music package, and then downloaded their favorite songs. Next they discovered how to send e-mails and load addresses.

A mutual friend, Julie, came over one day when they were together, and told them about the Social Media, and particularly about Facebook and Twitter. They eagerly downloaded those apps and began to add friends in both.

Meghan excitedly told her parents about the Social Media she had discovered, and neither of her parents were familiar with them, other than hearing about them once in a while in conversations.

Over a week or so they both seemed to add most of their friends at school to these apps, and were having fun texting and sharing everyday events with their friends.

As what usually happens in seventh grade, boys and girls begin noticing the opposite sex and some even had had boyfriends and girlfriends since being in the fifth grade, but those things never seem to last very long, and change quite regularly.

A new boy moved into their neighborhood that was their age and ended up in their class. He was a particularly good-looking boy named Tom Keller, and they both took a liking to him. When they realized they were both interested in Tom, there soon became a competition between them for his attention and things began to heat up between these close friends.

They began to have arguments about who Tom liked more, and even went as far as to calling each other names, and making fun of each other. Of course, Tom had no idea any of this was going on as the girls kept their arguing about him to themselves.

Soon Tom, who lived on the same street as both girls, began walking home with them after school. They all three became friends, but the competition for Tom continued between the girls without him having any idea about it.

The school was having its annual Thanksgiving Day Festival, where they had the gymnasium filled with different games and booths to raise money for the current school project. Families and students would come and play the games, like throwing a baseball to knock down three bottles stacked up, and win a prize. They also had cake walks, ring tosses, face painting, and the like for the fun of the crowd and to raise the money they needed.

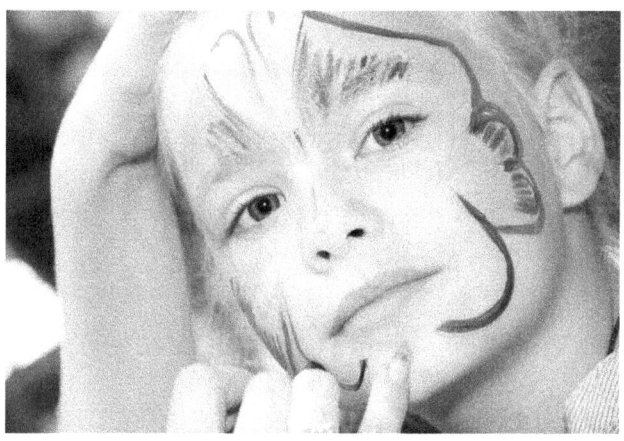

Tom asked Meghan to go to the Festival with him, and Susan was hurt. Since all three had become friends, she saw no reason for Tom not to take them both. The more she thought about it, the more upset she became. Her refusal to understand that Tom may prefer Meghan over her made her mad; in fact she became livid **(livid—furiously angry)**. She didn't realize that her anger was really a result of her feelings being hurt, but she foolishly wanted to hurt back.

As Susan thought more and more about the situation, she kept focusing on untruths like Meghan had purposely arranged this, or that Tom was being fooled by Meghan going after him, so Susan wouldn't have a chance with a relationship with Tom and so on, and so on. Her jealousy of Meghan became so strong that she began to think of ways to hurt her back. Meghan did nothing to hurt Susan purposely, nor did she realize that all of this was going on with her best friend, because Susan was hiding her feelings.

Susan decided to make up a disparaging story about Meghan and post it on her social media. She made up the story that Meghan was a shop-lifter who stole from the local stores, and then posted it on her social media to her friends. She never realized that once posted you can't take it back, and that the damage caused can be forwarded to many more people who were friends of her friends.

(*Disparaging—to describe someone or something as unimportant, weak, bad, and hurt their reputation)

When someone lies, they find out usually that one lie leads to another, and another as questions are asked. Soon Susan's friends began to ask Susan if this was true, and she had to lie and say yes to keep herself from looking bad for posting this untruth. Many of them were surprised, not only because Meghan was Susan's best friend, but because of that, they were surprised that Susan would post it about Meghan.

As the story gained momentum, Susan began to realize that she had really done something terrible. She also began to realize that when the truth came out it would be her reputation that would be ruined because of all of the lies, especially making up such a story about her friend.

Well, it didn't take long for this to get back to Meghan. Even though Susan had made sure she did not send the post to Meghan, she began to hear about it from everyone else. At first she thought it was a joke someone had started, until one of the girls pulled her phone out and showed Meghan the post by Susan.

Looking at the untruthful post had a numbing effect on Meghan. Then, as the reality of how many people were now seeing this about her and not knowing it is a lie, it began to sink in. Meghan was crushed to her very soul to know that her best friend had stooped so low as to publish this terrible untruth about her. She went home in despair and locked herself in her room crying.

Her parents knocked on her door asking to be let in, so she opened the door. They asked her what was wrong and she began to tell them what had happened. Her father became quite angry at first, but after calming down he told Meghan he was going to speak to Susan's father about this.

He went downstairs and as he opened the front door, he found Susan and her father getting ready to knock. Susan's father asked if they could come in and Meghan's dad told them of course. Susan was clinging to her father and sobbing because she had realized how this must have hurt her best friend and was afraid to face her.

Meghan's dad asked them to have a seat in the living room, and went upstairs to see if Meghan wanted to come down to hear what they had to say. Meghan had let her hair down and was brushing it when her dad came in the room. At first she said no, and then decided it had to be done sooner or later so she went with her dad.

As they entered their living-room, Susan put her head down in shame and was afraid to look at Meghan. Susan's father began to say that his daughter had come to him about this horrible thing she had done and wanted to do whatever she could to correct the matter.

He explained that he knew very little about this social media stuff, but had figured out that a posted confession by his daughter about her lies would be a good start. He furthered stated that he had taken her smart phone, and she would not get it back until she was much older and could understand the damage these things can cause to people.

Susan looked up and caught Meghan's eyes. She began to cry saying, "Meggie I am so sorry for all that I did, and have no excuse at all. I was jealous that Tom asked you to go to the festival with him, and felt hurt and wanted to get back at you for something that was never your fault. Can you ever forgive me?"

It turns out that Meghan had recently had a Sunday school class at church about the importance of forgiveness, and it had really made an impression on her. She stood up and said sternly, "Susan you need to post the confession about all of this right away, and make sure you confess to people asking about the lies you told."

Susan realizing that it looked like Meghan wasn't going to forgive her just lowered her head and said, "of course I will". Then, surprisingly to Susan, Meghan said, "And of course I will forgive you, you're my best friend and we all make mistakes. With that Susan ran to Meghan sobbing, and they hugged each other, Susan kept saying how sorry she was while Meghan said, "I know, I know".

Meghan's dad sat back with a very proud look on his face for his daughter's decision, while Meghan and Susan went running up the stairs to Meghan's bedroom to discuss other events going on in their lives.

The best friends were reunited through the power of forgiveness, and another of life's hard lessons was learned. If you lie in a way that hurts people, it will never go away until resolved. Many of the best friendships people have had were destroyed by lies and jealousy.

MORAL OF THE STORY

Untruths, better known as lies, can not only hurt and damage the person being lied about, but usually end up causing lie after lie to cover up the first one. This will hurt and damage the liar much more than the victim of the original lie.

Forgiveness for lying may not come as easy or at all as it did in Meghan and Susan's story, and even if it does come, there are usually harsh consequences to the liar.

STORY 3

THE STORY TELLER

Bill Cook was a boy who grew up feeling lonely. Maybe he felt that way because it seemed like he was not getting much attention from his parents, and others seemed to ignore him due to his shyness. As he grew older he was always making up stories that weren't true for the purpose of getting some attention. Some of his stories were quite unbelievable, and when found out to be not true, he gained the reputation of nothing but a story teller.

His story telling began at age four when he would call for his mother in an urgent tone and tell her things like there were animals under his bed, or he had seen someone in his closet, or a bear was in the backyard.

Once in school Bill felt left out on the playground and with the neighborhood kids. The main reason was Bill's shyness causing him to stay to himself, or mostly on the sidelines of the kids' activities. He wanted to participate with the other kids but didn't know how to go about it, so he found himself continually watching from afar.

Bill decided the way to get some attention was to make up things the other boys would be interested in, and try to have them get involved with him in looking into them. He never thought about what would happen when they found out he was lying.

One day, several of his classmates in his neighborhood were in a vacant lot throwing the football around. Bill went running up to them telling them he had just seen a small alligator in the area of the creek where the water pooled. This small pool the creek formed made a good swimming hole in the summer for the kids.

They all began with the "you did not, and no way" sayings until they saw the excitement Bill was showing. Then it was "let's go" as they all caught on to the excitement of the story, and began to run down the street, through the field and down the hill to the creek. They then ran down along the creek to the area where the water created a deeper pool where they had their swimming hole. They excitedly asked Bill where he had seen it, and was it on the shore or in the water.

Bill quickly said that he had seen it floating along in the swimming hole. With that the questions began, "Well where exactly?", and "can they stay under water long?", and "where do you think it is?"

Jimmy and Dan picked up some rocks and began throwing them into the swimming hole area trying to bring it to the surface. Sam got a long stick and started prodding the water. Jimmy said, "Are you sure it was an Alligator?" Bill shook his head yes. "How big was it?" asked Sam. "I don't know, maybe ten feet long", Bill answered. "Ten feet long, give me a break", said Dan. "If it was that big we would sure be able to see it in this shallow hole", said Jimmy.

The boys began to realize that Bill was not telling the truth about this whole thing, and they became annoyed with him. "What are you trying to prove with this phony story?" asked Dan. "Yeah, why did you bring us down here with this lie?" Jimmy said. "Maybe it got away", Bill tried to suggest, attempting to get himself out of this big whopper of a story.

With that the three boys turned and left Bill and headed back to the vacant lot. On the way they talked about what was wrong with Bill to tell such a tale, and made comments about what a jerk he was, and wondered why he was always making up stories that were never true.

Bill felt bad at what he had done, and just couldn't believe he had made up such a story. He walked home wondering what he was going to do about this big lie, and how he was going to get out of what he had told the guys.

The next day in school the boys ignored him even more, and when they did make eye contact, they just sort of shook their heads and then went on about what they were doing. Bill realized he had really done it this time, and just stayed to himself.

Every once in a while one of the boys would ask him if he had seen anymore alligators lately. Any of the other classmates in earshot would ask what alligators, and they would tell the story giving Bill a bad reputation for his lie. Bill went on for weeks feeling very sad about his doing this, and thinking he was never going to get out of it, or even that the boys would just finally let it pass.

One late spring day, Bill was back down at the creek by himself walking along the water when he heard a cry for help. He looked down the creek and the little rope bridge that had been there for years had broken, and a girl in her teens was laying in the creek, half in and half out of the water.

The rope bridge had broken when she was crossing and she fell a short fall but hit her head on one of the rocks and was very woozy. "Help me", she said faintly to Bill as he ran to where she was. Bill tried to take her arms and pull her out of the water but didn't have the strength to get her out. "Please help me, I can't move", she pleaded with Bill as he was trying to decide what to do.

"I'll be right back with help", Bill said to her, "It'll be alright, I'll be right back", he continued as he then got up and ran for help. Bill was very scared for the girl as he saw some blood on her head, and didn't know how bad she was.

Bill's parents weren't at home and he knew he had to find some help fast. As he ran up the hill, through the field and down the road he saw some of the boys in the vacant lot throwing a baseball.

He ran up to the lot and saw it was Jimmy, Dan, and Sam that were playing ball. Bill ran up to them and excitedly said, "Guys, quick come with me, there's a girl hurt down at the creek. The rope bridge broke and she fell and hit her head on a rock", he said breathlessly from the running.

"Yeah, right and I suppose the alligator is about to eat her too", said Sam as he obviously didn't believe a word of it. "Don't you ever learn?" asked Jimmy completely skeptical of what he was being told.

Still trying to catch his breath Bill said, "No, really, I'm not lying; she is hurt and I tried to pull her on to the bank but couldn't". "She is bleeding from her head, and said she can't move. You've got to believe me", he hurriedly told them in a panic to get the girl some help.

Dan noticed something different in Bill's demeanor and said, "Wait a minute, I think he's telling the truth". Both the other boys looked at him and said, "Ok, but if this is another one of your whopper's you're going to pay for it".

(demeanor—a person's appearance or behavior)

They all four began the run back down the road, across the field and down the hill to the creek. They quickly found the young teen girl just as Bill had said. "Quick, let's get her out of the water and on to the grass", Bill said taking control. "Jimmy put your sweater over her to try and keep her warm, and I'll run back up and get someone to call the paramedics", Bill said now handling the situation well. "You guys stay with her till I get back", Bill said.

Bill was very tired for making the run to the guys and back, but his adrenaline was flowing with the danger of the situation, and he just ran as fast as he could to get help.

(Adrenaline—a substance that is released in the body of a person who is feeling a strong emotion (such as excitement, fear, or anger) and that causes the heart to beat faster and gives the person more energy)

Bill was gone about fifteen minutes as he had caught one of the neighbors in her yard and had her call 911 for help, and then ran back down after directing the neighbor where to send the paramedics. The boys could hear the siren in the distance and knew help was on the way.

The paramedics arrived soon, and began checking the girl's injuries. First they put a brace around her neck to stabilize it from moving, then cleaned and put a bandage on her cut head to stop the bleeding. They finally checked her legs which she told them she couldn't move.

Fortunately, they had brought a body basket with them, and carefully and slowly lifted her into it. The two paramedics then got on each side of her, and lifted the basket while starting a slow run for the ambulance.

The boys ran ahead leading the way back, to where there was now a small crowd of people trying to see what was going on. Some policemen arrived as well as a fire truck, and there was even a news truck there.

The crowd began to clap to let the paramedics know their gratitude for such quick service. They slowly lifted the girl into the ambulance, and she asked to see Bill.

"Thank you, ahh", "Bill" said Bill as she was trying to know his name. "Yes, thank you Bill, you may have saved my life" she said, as the paramedics closed the door of the ambulance and headed down the street with the siren and lights flashing.

The boys were ecstatic about what had happened and their place in helping rescue the teen girl. "Wow Bill, you sure handled that great", said Jimmy. "You're not kidding", said Dan, "you really did a great job". "Thanks", said Bill, "And thanks for believing me after that last episode. I don't know what caused me to tell such a big lie, but I'm sorry".

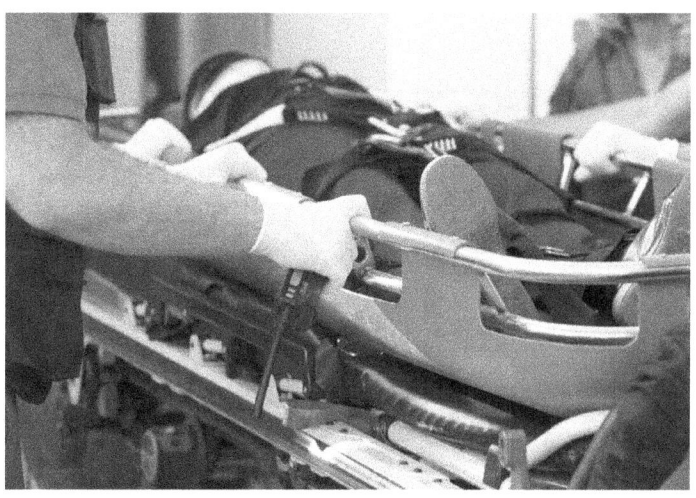

"That's Ok dude, you are forgiven", said Dan.

About that time the local news people came up to the boys and asked them what had happened. The other boys were quick to point out that if it hadn't been for Bill, she might still be down there. They asked Bill on camera about his heroism in saving the girl, and he simply said, "I could have never done it without the help of my friends here", as he stood with Jimmy, Dan and Sam. "We did it together", Bill stated, as they all four turned and walked on back down the road together.

> **MORAL OF THE STORY**
>
> It never pays to make up stories and lies about things. Once others hear them and find out they are not true, you can be labeled a liar and no one wants to hear any more from you. Then, when something serious happens it is difficult to get anyone to believe you, which could end up very badly.
>
> Here, Bill was able to convince his friends to help him before it was too late. If they had walked away from him what might have happened to the hurt girl in cold water?

STORY 4

ALWAYS BIGGER AND BETTER

Gary Adkins was a boy that always seemed to be in trouble. One of the reasons was he would lie about everything and anything to get attention, or attempt to keep himself out of trouble. Whenever anyone would talk about something they did, he had also done it, and more, bigger and better than the person telling the story.

Carol Grant was in Gary's class, and one day for an exercise, their teacher Mrs. Hearsom, asked if anyone in the class would like to tell of something that they did over the Spring break. Several raised their hands and Carol was picked to tell her story.

Carol stood up and was asked to come to the front of the class. She began about the Cockatiel bird her parents had bought her, and how these birds could talk. She explained that it really takes working with them regularly before they can learn a word or two, but she had managed to teach Dimple, her bird's name, several words over the break.

One thing she taught him was to say "Kiss Carol, and make the kissing sound. Now he would say it every time she entered her room like, "Kiss Carol, Kiss Carol, nch, nch, nch, nch, nch".

She went on to say that she was teaching him to crow like a rooster, but so far he sounds like a car motor trying to start, "r-r-ra,r-r-r-a, r-r-ra", she mimicked. All the kids laughed and Carol took her seat.

Gary raised his hand, and as the teacher called on him, he blurted out that he had taught his bird all kinds of things, and that it took him no time at all. "Well that's great Gary, what kind of bird do you have", she commented. He had to think fast as he didn't know the names of most birds and he couldn't remember what Carol had called hers.

"It's a parrot", he said quickly. Mrs. Hearsom asked him if he wanted to tell the class what he had taught the parrot, but he just said "Well lots of stuff, you know the things people usually train parrots to say", he began, not having any idea what people train parrots to say.

A number of his classmates had been to Gary's house and knew he was lying. Several of them sort of mumbled under their breath's things like, "Yeah, right", or "You liar". Mrs. Hearsom asked them if they had something to say to which they answered, "No Ma'am". "Ok, then keep quiet", she said. "Ring" went the bell ending class for the day, and saving Gary from a very embarrassing situation.

Now the main problem with this story was not only that Gary had never taught his parrot to speak, but that he had no parrot at all. Also when school got out the lies got worse. Hal and Larry, the two boys making the comments in class came up to Gary and said, "What a liar, you don't have a parrot!" Gary responded, "Yes I do, how would you know anyway? "Did you forget we've been to your house?" asked Larry. "You guys haven't been over in a couple of weeks, and we got the parrot since then", exclaimed Gary. "Oh really", said Hal, "Well let's all go over and see it, and you can show us what you taught it". "Well I'd like to, but I have a dentist appointment right now after school, and I've got to be going", Gary said as he turned from the boys and headed out.

Gary had no parrot and was telling a bold face lie to his teacher and class, and he also lied about teaching it words in a short time to make it sound like he was better than Carol in teaching her bird. He then repeated both lies when his classmates approached him outside about it, and then lied to their face about having a dentist appointment in order to get out of taking them to his house to show them something that was not there.

> **MORAL DILEMA**
>
> The consequences for bold face lies are that you have to tell more lies to cover the last one. They have to end somewhere because the teller will either get caught, or must be smart and apologize for telling such whoppers, ending the lying in the proper way.

Gary got home and went into his room and tried to think of a way out of it. He realized he could only buy some time with more lies, but eventually his classmates would find out the truth.

The first thing he did was ask his parents at dinner if they could get a parrot for a pet. "I'll take care of it, and even teach it to talk", he said. His mother replied, "Oh no, birds are very messy and require a lot of attention, and I don't have the time!" "No Mom, I said I will take care of it", Gary replied. "Oh sure you will, when it's convenient for you, then it falls on me", she said. "Gary, it doesn't matter because parrots are hundreds of dollars, and we don't have that kind of money for any bird, now or ever", his Dad chimed in.

Gary now saw that his bright idea to get himself out of his mess with lying was not going to work. He kept on thinking about it, and finally realized what he was going to have to do to get things straight. He realized that it was going to be very difficult for him, but it was the only way.

The next day he went up to the teacher before class, and hem hawed around trying to get the words out.

(Hem Haw—to pause a lot, and avoid saying something directly)

He finally told her that he had lied about the parrot story, and was sorry. "I don't know why I said what I did, but I did and I'm sorry", he told her.

His teacher looked at him with compassion and said, "Gary maybe the reason you always seem to have a bigger and better story than others is that you think it will make you look better to those who hear it. You should know that is not true", she explained. "All that does is make people think that anything you have to say is a lie", she continued.

(Compassion—sympathetic consciousness of others' distress together with a desire to alleviate it)

"You know Gary, you have a lot on the ball and you don't need to make up stories to have people like you. Just be yourself and you will do just fine", she concluded.

She went on to tell him that she accepted his apology, but he had lied to the whole class, and would need to tell them also. He knew she was going to say that, and didn't want to do it, but had decided he needed to get out from under the weight of the lies he had told.

The bell rang and Mrs. Hearsom said, "Class, Gary has something to say to you". Gary, still at the teacher's desk looked out above the class and said, "I want to apologize for telling you that I had a parrot I had taught words to", he began. "I don't have a parrot and I'm not sure why I said I did". He continued, "Carol, I'm sorry I tried to try to outdo your story, and Hal and Larry I'm sorry I continued that after school".

Gary's knees where shaking as he started back to his seat. Mrs. Hearsom told the class, "even though Gary should never have told these lies, it takes a big person to stand up and admit he has done wrong. I hope you will all forgive him". In order to get the air cleared quickly for Gary, she continued right away, "Ok take out your history books, and turn to page 103".

> **MORAL OF THE STORY**
>
> Bold face lies are told when people know they are not true. Gary had told his lie without thinking about his class friends who had recently been to his house and knew he didn't have a parrot. When they approached him, he had to make up another lie to cover the first, and so on.
>
> Telling the truth is the only way in life to keep straight and morally sound.

STORY 5

NEVER ADMITTED DOING WRONG

Jenny Traver could never understand why no one ever seemed to want to be around her. She was just like the other kids who liked video games, texting, ice skating, and playing softball, but no one ever called her; she had to call and invite herself along.

It was Saturday in the winter, and the school had a small skating rink where many of the people in the neighborhood liked to go and do some ice skating. The night before, it had snowed an inch or so, and the ice would have to be shoveled to make the skating better.

Early Saturday morning, Jill Linder, one of the girls in Jenny's class took her shovel and went on her own to shovel the snow off of the skating area behind the school. It took her an hour or so, and when she was done she was cold and tired, and went home to warm up and get some breakfast.

Ice skating was popular in this northern Ohio town during the winter, and about ten-thirty people began to show up, some with shovels expecting to have to remove the snow before skating. Jenny was one of the first to show up, and when the others got there and saw the snow already shoveled to the side, they asked Jenny if she did it.

"Yeah", said Jenny, "I came early to clear it off so we could all skate". "Well great, thanks for the hardwork. We were going to do it but it's sure nice that it's done already" said one of the guys who had brought his shovel.

After Jill had her lunch, she put her skates over her shoulders and headed back to the school rink. By that time a number of people were there, and one of her friends Karen, told her that Jenny had shoveled the snow earlier to clear the ice.

Jenny didn't know who had done the shoveling when she took credit for it, and when Karen told Jill that Jenny had done it, she was angry. Jill said to Karen, "She did not! I came early to clear the snow, and there was no one else here to help me. After I got done I was cold and hungry, so I went home to warm up and get some breakfast".

The two girls both looked at Jenny in disgust, and instead of Jenny owning up and admitting she lied, she simply said, "Oh so what, get over it!" and went on skating like nothing had happened at all. She was completely unrepentant for her lie.

(unrepentant—showing no regret for one's wrongdoings)

Jill was not surprised that Jenny didn't own up to her lying, because she had had more of her lying situations before, and Jenny never apologized for anything when she would get caught. Her favorite expression was always, "Oh get over it", and then just going on like nothing ever happened.

The next day, Linda Johnson, a girl living across the street saw Jenny, and went out to talk with her. "Jenny did you know that Bo Hendricks took his Mom's car and drove it around the block while his parents were out shopping the other day?" she asked. Now Jenny didn't know a thing about it but answered, "Oh sure I did, and I happened to be with him when he did". "You were?" asked Linda who was quite skeptical having known of many lies Jenny had told before.

(Skeptical—not easily convinced; having doubts or reservations)

Linda made a bad decision and decided to bait Jenny to try and have her caught in her lie.

(bait—to attract or catch)

"Did you also know he got caught and was grounded for a month by his father?" Linda asked. "Yeah, I knew that, tough luck for him", Linda replied. "Well at least his parents are going to let his friends see him at his house", Linda continued with her ruse.

(Ruse—a trick or act that is used to fool someone)

"Great, I think I'll go and see him", Jenny said.

> **MORAL DILEMMA**
>
> It is never right to use one lie to correct another. "Two wrongs never make a right" Linda was wrong in doing this.

On the way to Bo's house Jenny thought she would try to get Bo to tell others that she was with him when he drove his parent's car. She knew if he would, it would cover her lie to Linda.

Jenny arrived at Bo's house and knocked on the door. Bo's Dad came to the door and Jenny said, "I heard that Bo was grounded for driving his Mom's car around the block the other day, and I just wanted to see if I could see him to cheer him up".

Bo's Dad looked at Jenny in unbelief. Just as he was about to say something Bo walked up from the side yard. He had been out sledding on the big hill at the end of the neighborhood, and was coming home for lunch. "Hi Jenny", Bo said not realizing what was going on.

"Bo's Dad looked at Bo and said, "It seems that Jenny heard you were grounded for taking Mom's car around the block while we were gone the other day". With that, Bo's countenance changed quickly.

(Countenance—a person's facial expression)

"Well, I, uh, I mean that", he started to say. Jenny realized that she had really done it now with all of her lying.

"Well, I can see from your reaction we have something to talk about", his Dad said. "Driving at twelve years old is unlawful and unacceptable. You are in real trouble", his Dad continued. "Get in this house", his dad commanded. Bo dropped the rope to his sled and looked at Jenny with an evil stare, as he walked past his Dad and into the house.

"Who told you this?" Bo's dad asked Jenny. "Linda Moore", came Jenny's quick response. "Ok, I'll be speaking with her parents", Bo's Dad said as he closed the door. Jenny knew this was going to turn out bad.

After Bo's Dad spoke to Linda's parents, and they had found out from Linda that she told the truth about Bo driving the car, but later lied to Jenny to get her in trouble, they punished her. "Lying is never acceptable", Linda's father told her. "But Jenny lies all of the time and always seems to get away with it. I wanted to teach her a lesson", replied Linda to her Dad.

"It's not your place to teach Jenny a lesson", said her father. "Now look what's happened, he continued, "Bo may be getting what he deserved for doing such a foolish thing, but now you're grounded for lying". "Yeah, and Jenny gets away with her lies again", Linda complained.

In the meantime, Jenny had decided she needed to head off the trouble she thought was coming. She went to her parents and lied to them about the situation. "Believe me I had nothing to do with this at all, she said to her parents.

Unfortunately for Jenny, her Dad was best friends with Linda's Dad. He called Linda's Dad and found out about all of the lying going on by both girls, and confronted Jenny about it.

"Mr. Johnson told me the whole story Linda", he began, "about how she baited you with a lie about Bo being caught and grounded for his driving", he continued, "and Linda told her dad the reason she tried to trap you was because you are always lying, and always getting away with it. Well no more, you're grounded for a month and I'll decide what else you're going to get", her dad finished.

"No, he's lying Dad, I had nothing to do with this", she claimed again. "Ok Jenny, Linda's Dad is now lying. Do you expect me to believe that? You are grounded without cell phone or TV", said Jenny's Dad, "for not owning up to what you did. And if I hear of or catch you lying again, there will be more severe consequences! Do you understand me young lady?" he asked.

Without waiting for his daughter to respond he said, "Jenny you'd better realize that no one wants to be around a liar. People know they can't trust a liar, and if they can't trust you, they will never want to be your friend", her Dad said, "and you'll be left out."

"I didn't do anything wrong", Jenny insisted. "Well, you better think about that before it's too late", her Dad said, as he picked up her cell phone and closed the door of her room.

Back in school word got around about Jenny even lying to her dad and never admitting she had done wrong. As a result, her classmates would have nothing to do with her. Jenny became isolated.

(Isolated—separate from others)

She just couldn't seem to understand what the big deal was because she lied a little bit.

MORAL OF THE STORY

Would you want to be a friend or around someone you couldn't trust? Jenny was an unrepentant liar in that she would never admit she had lied or done wrong. As a result, she was punished, and should have had the answer to her earlier question of why it seemed no one wanted to be around her. When a person begins lying, they find they have to lie repeatedly to cover up the last lie. Eventually they will get caught and face consequences.

STORY 6

BACKED INTO A CORNER

Kerry Peters was an eleven year old boy and well-liked by his friends and classmates. He had a great personality and always seemed to get along with everyone. He was on the honor role in his sixth grade class, and helped out with the bulletin boards in his room to assist his teacher, Mrs. Kraft.

"Kerry, after math tomorrow, will you help me get the Spring bulletin boards up?" she asked. "I have some cut-outs I have put together to decorate the boards for Spring, and I could sure use your help", she said. "Sure, I'd be glad to. I'm just finishing up the one for science class", he replied "Thank you, you always do such a good job. I really appreciate it", she said.

Kerry went home that afternoon and threw the football with his older brother, and then they went in for dinner. He did his homework after dinner, and watched some television before going to bed.

The next day after math class, Kerry went and got the materials from Mrs. Kraft and began working on the bulletin boards. He was using the big pair of sharp scissors to cut out a large picture he was going to put up. The big scissors were awkward to use and very sharp, but worked well to cut out the big pictures and saved a lot of time.

He was working on the large bulletin board that was alongside the coat rack built into the wall. Kerry was lost in his work and wasn't paying attention when he swung around, and the large scissors slipped and made a gash in James Readings new leather coat that he got last Christmas. His first reaction was one of guilt for the coat being damaged, but it was just an accident. He slowly looked around and no one seemed to have seen what had happened to the coat.

Kerry knew how much James like that leather coat, and became afraid to tell him he made the gash in it. He continued finishing up the bulletin board quickly and then put everything away, taking his seat like nothing had happened.

The bell rang for the end of classes, and everyone put their things away and went to get their coats. James didn't notice the gash at first, and he swung the coat around his shoulders while putting it on.

"Hey James, what happened to your coat", asked Will Benson who had noticed the gash in his sleeve. "What do you mean?" asked James, "What gash?" Then as Will pointed to his sleeve, he looked down and saw it. It was about three inches long on his left sleeve, and he was upset. "What the heck happened to that", he asked unsuspectingly.

Some of the boys in including Kerry gathered around James as he said, "Well I sure didn't do it. I'd have known about catching it on something, or feel it tear", he stated. "Great, now my parents are going to be upset with me thinking I was careless with it", he said.

"Do any of you guys know what happened?" he asked the group around him. "I sure don't know", said Will, "I can't imagine what happened." "Hey Kerry, you were working over by where James' coat was hanging", said Chuck, another of the boys in the group, "Did you see anything?"

> **MORAL DILEMMA**
>
> Answering that he knew now would make Kerry look bad because he had never told James right when it happened as he should have. Now he felt backed into a corner.

Kerry felt like he was cornered and was confused about what to do. He hadn't done it purposely and it was an accident he couldn't foresee, however an expensive coat of his good friend had been damaged by him and he had to make a decision. He couldn't believe what came out of his mouth next.

"No, I didn't see anything. I was too busy putting up the cutouts Mrs. Kraft had given me", he said, but not without looking somewhat guilty.

Kerry was a good guy, but he failed to tell the truth because it would make him look bad. However, his body language was making it look like he knew more than he was saying.

(body language—can include body posture, gestures, facial expressions, and eye movements that can give away clues)

"Kerry, why do you look like that?" asked James sort of laughing, "you almost look like you did it"; James said without a thought that Kerry had done it. Kerry was a good friend of James, and James never suspected Kerry might have done it for a moment.

"Well, I know my folks are not going to be happy when I get home and they see this", said James, as he started out of the classroom door with the guys following him; that is all but Kerry. Kerry remained back and was fighting within himself how to correct this terrible mistake he had made by not telling the truth. He was very troubled, but he remembered what his Father had always taught him, that honesty was the best policy.

He finally decided what he had to do. "Hey, wait up you guys", Kerry yelled after the other boys. He ran to catch up with them, and he reached out for James's arm getting him to stop.

"James, I accidently cut your coat when I was working on the bulletin boards", he began. "I was using those big scissors, and as I turned they slipped hitting the sleeve of your coat gashing it. I'm so sorry I didn't tell you when it happened, but I know how much you love that coat, and I was, well just afraid to tell you what I had done", he confessed. "I don't know what got into me, but I'm sure sorry". Kerry finished.

James looked at Kerry for ten seconds or so, which felt like a year to Kerry, then said, "Well you've done the right thing now, as you usually do, so stop worrying about it. I forgive you", James said.

"Now you'll probably have to come up with a way to pay for the repair, but it'll be Ok", he said putting his arm around his friend. "You know we all make mistakes", James said to Kerry and the other guys, "and the best way to deal with mistakes is to own up and fix the situation".

Kerry was glad to have such a good friend as James, and knew he would never be reluctant to tell the truth again.

> **MORAL OF THE STORY**
>
> Even the best of people can or have lied when their backs were up against the wall, so to speak. Always telling the truth is the best policy, and if we lie, we should go and correct the lie with the truth quickly. Otherwise the situation can only get worse, and much harder to deal with.

STORY 7

THEY NEVER HURT ANYONE UNTIL...

Samantha's Mother had recently lost some weight, and had just come home from shopping for some clothes for herself that would fit better. She and Samantha's Dad had an important party they were going to, and she wanted to look her best.

Samantha walked into her Mother's room while she was trying on clothes. Her Mother saw her and asked, "What do you think about this one Sam?" as she held the dress in front of her before the mirror. "I don't know, what you think?" was the response from Sam who didn't like the look of the dress for her Mother at all. "I like it, or of course I wouldn't have bought it", said her mother. "What do you think?" she again asked Sam in hopes of getting a positive response.

Samantha realized her Mother had just spent money on this dress, and although she didn't like it, she decided to give her mother what she wanted. "Oh, I think its great Mom", said Samantha. "Do you really", asked her mother again. "Yeah Mom, it looks great", answered Samantha. "Well I got to go over to Judy's house for a while", said Samantha as she walked out of her mother's room. "Ok, but don't be late for dinner", her mother yelled after her.

As Samantha headed over to Judy's, she felt kind of bad because she told her mother a lie about her dress, when he mother wanted her honest opinion. Oh well, she thought, it was only a little white lie.

> **MORAL DILEMMA**
>
> Being truthful is the only way to build one's integrity. "Little White Lies" are untruths and may come back with consequences.

When Samantha got to Judy's house, they went out on the back patio to talk. Samantha began to tell Judy about the lousy looking dress her mother had bought for a party, and that she lied to her when she had asked what she thought about it.

"I feel bad that I wasn't honest with Mom", said Samantha. "I should have told her the truth about my opinion". "Oh Sam, you're so square, it's no big deal to lie about things like that", Judy said.

Samantha knew many people who felt like that, and called it "Little White Lies", but somehow she knew it was wrong, and couldn't seem to shake the bad feeling about it, even with Judy's comments.

Just then Judy's mother called out to Judy and asked, "What are you two doing out there?" Her mother needed help moving a big bookcase in the living room, but Judy just thought she was checking on them. "We're right in the middle of coming up with a science project Mom", Judy called back. "Oh ok", her mother said turning back to the living room.

Samantha knew Judy had just lied to her Mom about something that also seemed like no big deal. As the two girls continued to talk, they heard a loud noise and then Judy's mother yelling in pain. Both girls jumped up and ran inside.

Judy's mother was on the floor with the top of the full bookcase on her foot, and it was obvious she was in real pain. "Mom, what happened", she asked in a panic. Her mother answered in pain filled words, "I was trying to move the bookcase over a few inches, and the top section slipped off and hit my foot".

"Mom, why were you doing that yourself? Why didn't you ask us to help?" Judy asked. "Well I tried, but after finding out you two were in the middle of a science project, I thought I could do it myself without bothering you", answered her mother.

Judy and Samantha were both stung by her mother's answer. Judy had lied to her mother, just a little white lie that had now caused this painful injury to her mother. Judy began to cry as she could see the pain her mother was in, and blamed herself for the problem. "Oh Mom, I'm sorry, we could've helped, we were just fooling around outside" she sobbed, "we weren't working on a science project, I thought you were just checking on us", she said.

'Well don't think about it now", her mother said, "Call your Dad and ask him to come get me and take me to the emergency room", she said while trying fight the pain.

Judy ran to her phone and called her Dad, who was there in fifteen minutes. He carefully helped his wife to the car and took her to the doctor. Judy's mother had a small cut and a broken bone in her foot, but was alright.

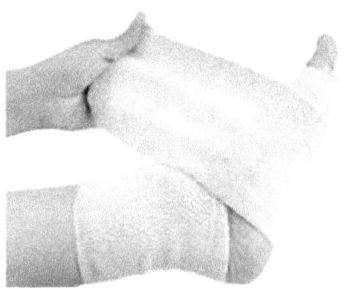

When her parents came home she apologized for the lie, and her Dad explained to her that any untruth, no matter how "White" it may be, can result in consequences that are hurtful. He made sure his daughter understood she was always to tell the truth.

Samantha went home and apologized to her mother. "Mom, I'm sorry I lied to you when I told you I liked your dress. I thought it was just a little white lie in not wanting to hurt your feelings, but have since become aware that the truth is always the best way to go. Please forgive me".

"I do forgive you Sam, and you're right, no matter whatever the situation is, always be truthful. If you are worried about hurting someone's feelings, you can tell the truth in different ways", her mother continued. "You could have said something like Mom, that wouldn't be my first choice, which would convey your feeling without lying", she explained.

"Sam, you can always find the right thing to say without having to lie. Just remember there is no such thing as a white lie, only a lie" her mother told her.

"Thanks Mom, I understand and have learned a good lesson today".

> **MORAL OF THE STORY**
>
> Judy learned the hard way why telling any kind of lie, even what seems like a small one, can have serious consequences you can't foresee. Sam had her bad feeling about her lie confirmed when she saw what happened to Judy's mother.

STORY 8

LYING TO MY PARENTS IS NO BIG DEAL

Craig Dalton and his friend Joe Fisher were on their way out of the house one afternoon, when his mother met them at the front door. "Craig where do you think you are going", his mother asked him. "Oh just down to play some "hoops" Mom", was his quick response. "No sir mister, you have not done your chores yet, and they will all be done before you go anywhere", she commanded. "Mom, I finished my chores already, and I have to go because our game is about to start", he said.

"You're telling me all of your chores were done in the last hour, because they weren't before that?" she asked him. "Yeah mom, all done", he said. "We'll you wait here while I check", Mrs. Dalton told him. Just then the phone rang and Craig's mom began talking to her best friend, and just waived Craig on, so off they went. "Well that was easier than I thought", said Craig as he and Joe ran out and across the field.

As they got far enough away and slowed down, Joe said to Craig, "I can't believe you just lied to your Mother. What's going to happen when she finds out?" he asked. "Oh Mom will probably forget about it after her call. It's usually Dad who checks on jobs being done, and he's out of town", Craig responded. "Man, if I lied to my parents I wouldn't see daylight for two weeks", Joe told Craig.

The two boys arrived at the park where their other friends were shooting basketball until they got there. "What took you so long?" Jimmy asked. "I had to do my chores before I could get out", said Craig. Joe just looked at Craig in amazement as he had just told another lie. "Oh you didn't do your chores", Joe said, contradicting his friend. "Yeah, well I had to make it seem like I did so I could get here on time", retorted Craig, annoyed that Joe had given his lie away.

Sides were chosen and the game began, with Craig and Joe on different teams. During the game, Craig was trying to take the ball from a boy on the other team and the other boy outmaneuvered him. As that boy, Frank, passed the ball to a teammate, Craig shoved him so hard he fell and scraped his knee. Everyone stopped to see what happened.

"What do you think you're doing", said Frank, "that's a foul and you did it on purpose". "Oh I did not", Craig responded, "you just fell". The boy jumped up and shoved Craig saying, "You're a liar. You did that on purpose because I slipped around you when you went for the ball", said Frank. "You're full of it", Craig said back loudly.

Jimmy came up to both boys and said, "He's not full of it Dalton, we all saw it and you did shove him down on purpose", he said. "Yeah, well if he can't take a little hard B-ball, maybe he shouldn't play", retorted Craig. "No, if you can't play fairly and take the blame when you do something wrong maybe you shouldn't play", said Jimmy right back at him. "OK, Joe you saw it, tell them I didn't shove him down", said Craig.

MORAL DILEMMA

Joe had just been asked by his close friend Craig to lie for him to cover his lie. Joe was respected among his friends for his honesty, and was not going to have a friend make him a liar also.

"Craig, don't bring me into this", his friend warned. "No, you saw it so tell them what happened", Craig said, expecting his friend to back up his lie.

"Alright Craig, I'll tell what I saw. When Frank pulled around you while you were trying to get the ball and got away from you, you ran up and shoved him to the ground, that's what I saw", said Joe reluctantly.

Craig drew back in disbelief. He had been sure his close friend would back him up, but he didn't. He spoke out in anger, "Joe what makes you so lily white all of the time. I suppose you never do anything wrong", Craig asked.

No Craig, it's not that I don't do things wrong sometimes, it's that I own up to them when I do", responded Joe. "Now you want me to lie for you to cover your lie, and I'm not going to do that", said Joe, "and you should have known that about me by now", he continued. "Personally I think we should continue this conversation somewhere else", said Joe, trying to end this embarrassment for his friend.

"No, this conversation is over, and I'm 'outta here", Craig said angrily. Craig headed back to his house, muttering under his breath about Joe being some friend, and why these things always happened to him. He just couldn't seem to understand that he brought these things on himself with his lies.

When Craig arrived home, he was surprised to see his Dad's car in the driveway, meaning he was back early from his business trip. He ran into the house glad his Dad was back, and wanted to see him. "Hi Dad, glad you're home", said Craig to his dad. "Hello son, I'm glad to be home also, that is until I found out some things", his dad said slowly. "Why have you lied to your mother about having your jobs done when they haven't even been started", his father asked sternly.

Craig hung his head knowing he was no longer going to fool his dad. "I don't know, I was late for the game and didn't want to miss it", he said.

"Craig, I'm really getting tired of all of these lies you keep telling. You didn't do this when you did, or did do that when you didn't", his father sternly said. "We are going to put a stop to this now", his dad continued, "I hope you aren't doing this with your friends also. They will soon want nothing to do with you if you are, at least the ones worth having as friends", he said.

Craig thought of his friend Joe, and how he is always honest and truthful. He knows everyone loves that about him, and even if they do make fun of him sometimes for it, he always stands his ground.

"I'm sorry Dad", Craig said. "Well I hope you really are, but sorry won't do it. For the next month you are to come home directly after school, and do any chores your mom or I have for you. You can then have some time for yourself, at home of course, before you begin your homework. Weekends you will do extra things around the house. After two weekends, if everything has been done correctly with no lies, we'll see about the following weekends", his Dad said. "And Craig, the next lie I catch you in will double this punishment, so be very careful what you tell us", his dad finished. "OK Dad, I'll get this corrected", Craig said, with a new resolve to do it.

At school the next day Craig approached Joe and said, "Joe I'm really sorry for all of my lying, and especially trying to bring you into it with the guys the other day". Joe looked at his friend and said, "Craig, the fact you are admitting it goes a long way with me.

"Yeah, well my Dad got home early and caught me in the lies to my mother. I will have jobs to do every night after school and grounded from weekends for a couple of weeks, but I'm glad it happened; I know things were getting out of control", Craig said.

"It'll all be worth it", said Joe, "Trust me". After school the boys headed home together, and Craig was feeling much better for putting the lying behind him.

MORAL OF THE STORY

Craig, like so many others, get caught up in lying to cover themselves for what they have done, or what they have not done. He could see the respect Joe always had because he was always honest, and people knew they could trust him.

Being truthful is one of the most important traits a person can have, because people notice it, and the integrity of the honest person makes it much easier to get ahead in life.

GOOD MANNERS MAKE YOU THE POSTER CHILD FOR SMART

STORY 9

WHY DON'T PEOPLE LIKE ME?

Bobby Lands is an eleven year old boy who is not unlike the other boys in his class, except for the fact he was often ignored and didn't seem to fit in. Bobby wanted to be liked and have friends but he was usually left out of recess games and after school activities, and couldn't understand why. As a result, his feelings were hurt and he had no idea why the other kids didn't seem to like him.

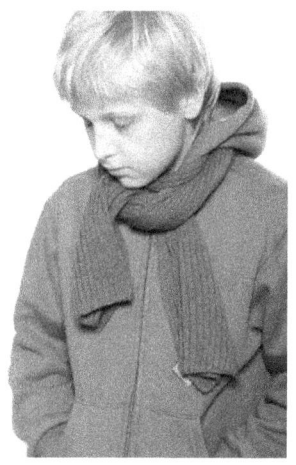

A classmate of Bobby's, Hal Unger is one of the popular guys at school, and also one of those who ignored Bobby. One day their science teacher assigned pairs of students to do a science project together, and have it done for the next week. She assigned Hal and Bobby to do their project together, which didn't make Hal very happy.

Hal got up from his seat and approached their teacher alongside of his desk. Hal whispered, "Mr. Smith can I do my project with Gary Kline? He is my best friend and I think we will work better together". Hal was trying to be quiet about it so Bobby wouldn't hear him. Mr. Smith, only thinking that Hal preferred to be with his friend said in a normal voice, "No, you and Bobby Lands will do this one together".

Bobby heard this, as did the rest of the class, and it seemed everyone turned to look at Bobby to see his reaction. Trying to maintain his cool, Bobby said loudly to the teacher, "It's OK Mr. Smith, he can do it with Gary", waiting for the teacher to respond. "No Mr. Lands, the selections will remain as I said. Mr. Unger, take your seat", said the teacher in an annoyed fashion.

Hal went back to his seat, and Bobby looked down trying to hide his embarrassment and hurt feelings. Once Mr. Smith had assigned all pairs of boys for the projects, he told all of the pairs to get together and decide what they wanted to do them on.

Much to Bobby's surprise, Hal walked over to him and said very nicely, "What do you think Bobby, do you have any ideas?" Now Hal Unger had rarely spoken to Bobby in the past, but now he was being very nice and friendly. "Uh, I don't know Hal, maybe we could do a space drawing or sculpture of some kind showing the positions of the other planets to the earth", offered Bobby.

"Hey, that's a great idea", said Hal, "you want to do it at my house or yours?" Bobby was almost dumbfounded, as he had never thought to be asked to Hal's house, and he was pleased at the offer. "Is your house OK?" Bobby asked meekly. "Sure, why don't you come over after dinner around seven this evening", Hal said. "OK, Hal, sounds good to me", Bobby responded.

On the way home, Bobby was excited about working on a project with one of the most popular guys in school. This was the first time in a long time that he felt he was being included, but was also trying to forget that Hal had asked for someone else when he was named to be his partner.

Bobby arrived at Hal's house with his big Astronomy Atlas book that he knew would give them the information about the planets location to the Earth. Hal seemed glad he had the Atlas, but was a little more reserved than he was at school.

As the boys opened the Atlas and began to make note of the different planets they wanted to use in the project, Hal noticed that Bobby really knew his stuff and he was amazed at his knowledge of space.

"I had no idea you were so smart about these things", said Hal. "As a matter of fact I never knew much about you at all", he continued. "Well I use most of my time after school studying, or playing video games", Bobby said. "I just never seemed to fit in with you all, and I always seemed to be left out in outside activities", he continued, "and I never knew why", he said. Then, stepping out in uneasy territory Bobby asked, "Do you know why Hal?"

Hal had been afraid that these kinds of questions might come up when he was paired with Bobby, and also felt uneasy about it, not wanting to say something that would hurt Bobby's feelings.

'Oh I don't know", Hal began trying to let this go away, but leaving a sense that he knew more than he wanted to say. "Common Hal, I need to know. I feel like I have missed out on so much, and don't know why", he explained.

Hal realized Bobby was more likeable and smart than he thought, or than the other guys thought, so he decided to help him. "Look, Bobby, this isn't easy for me to tell you, but here goes. The main reason I think you haven't fit in is your lack of being clean", he started. "Most of us have noticed for a long time that you always look dirty, and frankly smell like it also", he said. "The smell tells us that you haven't taken a bath in a while, and is just unpleasant to be around the odor. Have you noticed how the seats around you in class are usually empty?" Hal asked.

Bobby was embarrassed and a little surprised No one had ever said anything about this except his parents, and he always thought they were exaggerating. "I guess I never realized that about being clean and never realized I stank", Bobby said. "At least that explains why kids didn't want to sit near me. I though they didn't like me", he explained.

> **MANNERS NOTE**
>
> Good manners begin with cleanliness and good hygiene (Hygiene—the things that you do to keep yourself and your surroundings clean in order to maintain good health)

"I'm sorry to have to tell you this Bobby, but that's why I'm sitting across the table from you now. You usually have a foul odor coming from you, and it's not pleasant to be around", Hal said. "It has nothing to do with not liking you because people haven't gotten to know you. People don't want to be around bad smells", he said.

"And you can fix that easily", he explained. "Anyway, I'll get some poster board and we'll get back at it tomorrow night", Hal said, wanting to get out of this embarrassing situation.

"Ok Hal, we'll continue tomorrow night", Bobby said, and rather slowly while he was absorbing what had just been told him. Then he finally said, "Hal thanks, as embarrassing as that is to me, I'm really thankful you told me the truth. I will take care of that problem from now on", he finished.

Hal walked up to Bobby and said, "Bobby I tell you now, if you get that "being clean" thing taken care of, you'll see a big difference in the way people react to you, I guarantee", said Hal trying to encourage Bobby. "See you tomorrow", Hal said as Bobby went out of the door.

The next day Bobby came into class showered and with noticeably clean clothes on. Hal was talking to some of the guys and motioned for Bobby to come over to them. "Hey Bobby", said Hal breaking any ice that may have been hanging around. A couple of the guys noticing a change in Bobby also greeted him, and asked him if he would like to shoot some hoops with them on Saturday. Bobby was stunned and Hal interjected quickly, "Of course he'll join us", winking at Bobby.

From that day forward Bobby became one of the crowd, and had learned a good lesson in the manners of cleanliness.

MANNERS IN STORY

Politeness—Hal whispered to the teacher so as not to hurt Bobby's feelings

Cleanliness—Hal was honest with Bobby about being clean and not smelling when he was asked

Consideration—helping Bobby get into the group so they could all recognize his change.
What other manners can you name?

STORY 10

CHAOS AT THE FAMILY TABLE

(Chaos—a state in which behavior and events are not controlled by anything)

The Wilsons had a large family of five kids, ranging from one to 12 years old. There were two girls, Mary 12, Jan 5, and the three boys were John10, Bill 8, and Cade 1. The Wilsons always had dinner together at the family table, and doing so was a time of sharing and closeness for the whole family. However they did have times when things would get out of control with everyone wanting to add something or bring up something that had happened to them.

One evening the kids were off either playing or doing their homework. "Dinner" yelled their mom and the stampede started down the stairs. Mr. Wilson put down his paper and walked to the dining room saying in a loud voice, "Ok, slow down, slow down everybody. Did you all wash your hands?" he asked as a usual part of their pre-dining ritual. "John, hands washed?" he asked his son who was a constant offender. "Ok Dad, I'll wash 'em" John answered as he headed back to the bathroom.

Everyone else sat down at the table as Mrs. Wilson brought out the food. "Pass the potatoes" said Mary to whoever was near them. "Please pass the potatoes" her Dad sternly said, "is the way to ask for something, but nothing is to be passed until we pray" he told them. When Mrs. Wilson finally sat down, they all bowed their heads while their Dad asked the Lord to bless the food, and gave thanks for their dinner.

"Ok, now who wants some chicken" said Mrs. Wilson. "Me, me, me, I do" came several loud answers from some of the kids. "I want a breast", said Mary. "You always get the white meat", said Bill loudly, angry that Mary always took his favorite part of the chicken. "I do not" Mary responded.

"Yes you do" Bill argued back. "Well I never get anything but a wing and drumstick" said little Jan trying to get into the discussion. "Now wait a minute" said John sitting next to her, "I gave you a thigh last time and took the wing and drumstick myself because you complained then" he said. Older sister Mary decided she would enter the fray and said, "I think I'm just going to take it all", knowing she was going to make matters worse.

(Fray—a usually disorderly or protracted fight, struggle, or dispute)

"That's enough", their Dad shouted over all of their voices. Everyone became quiet because when their Dad shouted, he meant business. "Now this is a fine display of how not to act at the dinner table. What has happened to your table-manners your Mom and I have taught you for years? You shouldn't be able to eat at all if this is the way it goes", their Dad said sternly. "Now because of all this, we are going to review table-manners from the start as we eat dinner" he said more calmly.

"Ok, before we go a step further, what went wrong tonight first?" he asked. After a brief moment of silence for thought, Jan said, "John forgot to wash his hands before dinner". "Correct, and for that Jan, you get to have first choice of the chicken", her Dad told her.

"Thanks Dad, I want a thigh, but I want to give it to John because I know he likes that part" she said. "Jan I'm proud of you! Who can tell me what manners Jan just showed?" her Dad asked. "She is nice" Bill offered as Jan put a thigh on John's plate. "Ok, good Bill, but what else?" their Dad asked. "She was considerate!" said Mary, "by putting someone before herself" she said. "Good answer Mary" her Dad responded.

"Let's everyone get their food and eat while we discuss this", added Mrs. Wilson, "We don't want the food to get cold", she said.

"Since we're going to review proper table-manners, let's make a game out of it. If we get more than ten different table-manners in addition to the ones we had, we'll all go out for an ice cream cone for desert", their father said.

After several cheers from some of the family, Mary said, "Oh, I've got one. Before dinner I should have gone into the kitchen to asked Mom if she needed help putting the food out". "That's a good one Mary, and yes you should have, but that fits under consideration which we already have, so we can't count it as one of our ten", her Dad said.

"This is an easy one, but good manners tell us that there should be no shouting or arguing at the table", said John. "Very good John, there's one", said Mr. Wilson.

"Don't put your elbows on the table" offered Jan, while she noticed that Mary had put hers on the table. "That's right Jan, and Mary you might try that now", her Dad said with a laugh, "and that's two".

"At the table, there should be no slurping, burping, or humming" offered Bill. "Good, that's three" said their father. "Don't stuff your mouth or talk with your mouth full" said John, "and chew with your mouth closed" he added. "Those are excellent but we're only going to count them as one because they are about the use of our mouths" their Dad said, "So that's four", he added.

"Always say please and thank you" Jan recited, wanting to add her part. "Very good Jan, Thank you" her Dad said to her. "That's five!"

"Sit up straight at the table" recited Mary. "I've heard that many times" she added. "That's right, John", Mr. Wilson said looking at John who had slumped down in his seat. John sat right up and said, "Sorry". "Good one Mary now we at six" said her Dad.

The kids were thinking hard because they had four more to come up with, and they knew there were many more if they could just think of them.

"Wait for everyone to be served before eating" blurted out Bill, being please he had remembered another. "That's right Bill", said his Dad, and before praying too" he added. "OK, now we have seven and need only three more for the ice cream cones" he reminded them.

Jan raised her hand as they do in her kindergarten class, and her Dad said, "Ok Jan, do have one?" he asked. "Keep your napkin in your lap", she said sort of uncertainly. "Good one Jan", her Dad said. "Well if we're supposed to keep our napkins in our laps, why does Mom always tuck mine into my collar?" she asked. Her mother was sitting next to her and said, "We keep them in our laps once we get to a certain age Jan. When you're little it helps to keep food from spilling on your clothes, to tuck your napkin into your collar". "Oh" said Jan.

"Ok, two more everybody, so who's got another one", asked Mr. Wilson. "I know one", said Bill, "Don't reach for things at the table, but ask to have them passed", he said with a pleased look on his face. "Very good Bill, ok one more", his Dad said. There was silence for a moment, and their Dad repeated "Ok, one more, who has it" he asked.

"I know, we need to ask to be excused before leaving the table" stated John, and before his Dad could answer, he quickly added, "And can I be excused to get a free ice cream cone?" he joked.

Every one of the kids clapped with excitement for completing the game their Dad started, and were ready to go get their ice cream. "Very, very good everyone, you win the prize", said their Dad.

With that, Bill and Mary got up quickly to take their plates to the kitchen. "Uh, uh, uh", said their Dad. Knowing immediately what he wanted, they quickly sat back down and both asked to be excused. The others also chimed in asking to be excused and their mother said, "Yes and please take your dishes to the kitchen". Ten minutes later they all piled into their family SUV, and headed to the ice cream shop.

TABLE MANNERS IN THIS STORY

Wash hands before eating

Being considerate of others

No shouting or arguing at the table

Don't put your elbows on the table

No slurping, burping, or humming at the table

Don't stuff your mouth, or talk with your mouth full, and chew with your mouth closed

Always say please and thank you

Sit up straight at the table

Wait for everyone to be served before praying and eating

Keep your napkin in your lap

Don't reach for things at the table, but ask to have them passed

Ask to be excused from the table

STORY 11

THE SHORTSIGHTED NEIGHBORS

(Shortsighted—not considering what will or might happen in the future)

Lakeishia Veal lived a few doors down from Tania Brown, who had moved into the neighborhood during the summer. Both girls were ten and Tania would be in the same class as Lakeishia when school started back in the fall.

The girls became great friends and found they really liked many of the same things. The difference between them was that Tania had moved with her parents from Philadelphia with both of them working, while Lakeisha's mother was able to stay at home with her children. During the summer Tania was able to stay most days over at Lakeisha's house while her parents worked.

Lakeisha's mother was a warm and friendly woman, but in meeting Tania's parents she was surprised that they practically expected her to watch their daughter during the days in the summer without even asking her, which was not her responsibility. She decided she would say nothing to them unless it became a problem.

> **MANNERS NOTE**
>
> Tania's parents showed lack of good manners by expecting Mrs. Veal to watch their daughter. She was too young to stay alone at home, and they were expecting to use Mrs. Veal as an unpaid babysitter.

One afternoon the girls were playing outside and Tania decided to jump off of the porch, but landed wrong breaking her ankle. She screamed in pain and Lakeisha's mother came running out to see what had happened. She tried to comfort Tania, but she kept wanting her mother. "Lakeisha, go into the bathroom cabinet and bring me the Ace bandage on the shelf", Lakeisha's mother calmly told her daughter.

Tania was crying and asking for her mother while Mrs. Veal was wrapping her ankle with the Ace bandage. "Here, let me help you up Tania, and I want you sit on the steps until I get the car to take you to the emergency room", Mrs. Veal said.

"No, I want my mother", cried Tania being afraid of going to the hospital. "Don't worry dear; I'm going to call your mother first before we leave. Lakeisha, you stay here with Tania, until I make the call and get the car out of the garage", her mother told her. "Ok Momma", replied Lakeisha looking a little scared about what had happened to her friend.

Going into the house to call Tania's mother, Mrs. Veal realized that she had never given her the number to her office. She went out and asked Tania if she knew the number, to which Tania said no. "Ok, we'll just have to take you and call her later", said Mrs. Veal. "No", protested Tania in fear, but Mrs. Veal went down and hugged her and told her it would be alright, and that she would be with her the whole time. With that, Mrs. Veal went and backed her car out of the garage, and got out and helped Tania into the front seat.

In the emergency room, they took Tania to X-ray and Mrs. Veal went with her as promised. Later, the doctor came to her cubicle and told them that Tania had a broken ankle and he would have to put a cast on it. Tania cried out, "No", but Mrs. Veal rubbed her back and told her it would make her feel much better, and when they got home, they could have some ice cream.

Later that afternoon Tania's mother came home, and not seeing Tania outside or in the house, she walked over to Mrs. Veal's house. She knocked on the front porch door, and heard Tania call out loudly, "Momma". She went in as Mrs. Veal was coming to the door. "What's going on?" asked Mrs. Brown. Then she saw Tania on the porch swing with a cast on her foot.

Running over to her she said, "Oh my baby, what have they done to you?" She hugged her daughter and looked at Mrs. Veal in anger and said, "What did you do to my daughter?" Mrs. Veal began to say,

"Now, we have done nothing to your daughter she…" Mrs. Brown cut her off. "How could you let this happen to my poor baby girl", she snapped back. "Mrs. Brown, we didn't let anything happen to Tania. She jumped off the porch while the girls were playing and landed wrong, breaking her ankle", Mrs. Veal said beginning to get annoyed.

"Alright, we'll just have to see what my lawyer says about this', spouted out Mrs. Brown. "But Mamma, Mrs. Veal", Tania began to say before he mother cut her off and said, "That's enough, let's just get you home", Mrs. Brown told her.

Lakeisha's mother had had enough! "Now you listen to me Mrs. Brown, if any one has to worry about trouble with the law, it will be two parents who leave their daughter of eleven home alone all day every day. "Well, you're supposed to be watching her", snapped back Tania's mother.

"Since when", responded Mrs. Veal, "You never asked me to watch Tania, you just assumed I would with no consideration for me and what I may have to do during the days", she started. "Just where do you get off with those kinds of expectations? Have you no manners at all? Not a thought about food for your daughter, or what it might cost me all summer to feed Tania" she said. Then looking at Tania quickly and seeing her distress about all of this she said, "Don't you worry about this Tania, this is between your parents and I".

Then starting back at her mother, Mrs. Veal continued, "And you never even left a phone number for me in case of an accident like today. I went to call you and realized I had none, and when I asked Tania, she couldn't remember it. So I did what I had to do to take care of Tania by wrapping her ankle and getting her to the emergency room. And now you come to my house with your high and mighty attitude about something that is totally your responsibility? You have a lot of nerve", she finished.

Mrs. Brown, realizing everything that Mrs. Veal had said was true hung her head and began to cry. After a few moments, she looked up and said "Mrs. Veal I'm so sorry, I don't know what's the matter with me, I think it may be all of the pressure I'm under at work" she began. "I know that is no excuse for my behavior, and only hope you will forgive me for my complete lack of manners" she said. "I had no right to think that because you were at home you could watch Tania" she continued. Then she pulled Tania to her and looked back at Mrs. Veal and said, and here you have taken all of this time to take care of her, with the hospital and everything. Can you ever forgive me?" she asked.

Mrs. Veal looked at her daughter and then Tania and walked over and put her hand on Tania's shoulder saying, "Oh of course I forgive you. We all have stressful times in our lives, which causes us to act in a way quite different from our real selves" she said.

"Mrs. Veal", Tania's mom began to say, when Mrs. Veal interjected, "Gloria". "Thank you Gloria, and please call me Janice" said Tania's mother. "I promise you that I will brush up on my manners so my Tania will be able to have a good example instead of a bad one from me" she said.

From that day on Lakeisha and Tania's mothers became good friends. Mrs. Veal continued to watch Tania during the summer, and Mrs. Brown gave her money, after Mrs. Veal tried to refuse it, to compensate her for her time and food. Meanwhile, Lakeisha and Tania had learned by what they saw, a good lesson in manners.

MANNERS IN THIS STORY

Bad Manners

Expecting Mrs. Veal to take care of Tania without even asking or compensating her

Not leaving a phone number in case of emergency

Jumping to ridiculous conclusions when seeing Tania in a cast and accusing her of not taking care of her

Threatening Mrs. Veal with legal action before knowing what happened

Good Manners

Mrs. Veal taking care of Tania for Tania's sake

Comforting Tania when she was hurt and giving first aid

Taking Tania to the emergency room when she had no way to reach her parents

Forgiving Mrs. Brown for her attack and threatening her

Continuing to take care of Tania

STORY 12

JUST WHAT IS THE GOLDEN RULE

This Saturday was the day for registration for Little League Baseball in Centerville, Ohio. The boys had been talking about it all week at school, and the announcement they had made that the Ballpark had more kids expected to register this year, than they had scheduled games for them all to play. Reluctantly the Ballpark announced that it would have to be first come first serve, and some might not be able to play this year.

Registration would open at 9:00 am Saturday morning, and everyone was talking about getting there early so they would be able to get on a team. Kenny Sands and Larry Baskin were best friends, and were among the boys talking about baseball registration. Kenny was a natural at baseball, and wanted to be a baseball player when he grew up. Larry was an average player at baseball, but was quite good at basketball.

Early Saturday morning Kenny went into his parent's bedroom to wake his dad up for registration. He had forgotten to tell his dad about it, but his dad was always home on Saturday's, so he never thought about it. When he entered the room, his dad wasn't there so he woke his mom up asking where his dad was. "Oh, he had some business he had to do this morning" his mother answered. "Oh no", said Kenney, "baseball registration is this morning" he explained. "Well your dad will just have to do it when he gets home", his mother said. "Mom, they are expecting more kids than they have places for this year, and its first come, first serve" Kenny told his mother. "Honey I'm sorry, but we'll just have to see what we can do when your Dad gets home" his mother replied.

Larry and his dad were there early and Larry kept looking for Kenny wondering why he wasn't there yet. The man in charge had just announced that the registrations were almost filled, and the line was still back quite a ways from where Kenny was.

Meanwhile, Larry's dad went to get some coffee provided at the table that the Ballpark had set up, and while he was gone, Butch Gordon, a big boy came up from the back of the line, and cut in front of Kenny, to make sure he could register. "Excuse me Butch" Kenny said to the boy, "go back to where you were" he told him. "Why don't you try and make me" the boy told him. Now Butch was much bigger and heavier than Kenny so he knew he couldn't make him go back.

Soon the boy's father, who had also gone for coffee was walking up the line trying to find out where his son had gone. When he got up to him he said, "Son, what are you doing way up her? You can't just come up here and cut in line", his dad told him. "But Dad, I might not get to register back that far", his son pleaded. "That's because you didn't get up when I tried to wake you several times this morning", his dad replied.

With that he came out of line and walked back with his dad to where they had been. "Son it is bad manners to cut in line. Don't you remember the Golden Rule I taught you, "Do unto others as you would have them do unto you"? How would you like it if you were up there and someone cut in front of you?" his father asked.

Larry's Dad came back with his coffee, just about the time Larry got to the registration table. While he was filling out his form, he heard the man call out that registration was full and apologizing for all those in line who couldn't register. Larry thought about Kenny and hoped he had gotten their earlier to register.

When they got home, Larry ran over to Kenny's house to see if he had registered. Kenny's Mom answered the door and told Larry that he was up in his room. Larry ran up the stairs and saw Kenny moping around in his room. "I guess you didn't get to register", Larry stated. "Nope", said Kenny, "I forgot to tell my dad that today was the day and he left earlier on business", Kenny explained. "Oh man, that stinks", commented Larry. "I was hoping we would get on the same team" Larry said. "Yeah, me too", said Kenny, "and it's all my fault! I just can't believe I forgot to tell Dad", he said. "Look Larry, I have to do my Saturday jobs so I'll catch up with you later"

Kenny stated sadly. "Ok man, I'll catch you later" answered Larry, realizing Kenny was in no mood to keep talking about it.

When Kenny got back home, he went into the kitchen where his dad was reading the paper. "Dad, can I talk to you for a minute?" he asked. "Sure son, what do you have on your mind?" his father asked back.

"Kenny didn't make registration because he forgot to tell his dad it was today, and his father was gone on business", Larry started. "What would you think if I gave my registration to Kenny? Baseball is his thing, and basketball is mine", he said to his dad. "I only really wanted to play baseball if Kenny was going to too, but now, I really don't care about it", he explained.

"Well I think that would be a very fine thing to do for your friend" his Dad answered. "I'm aware that basketball is your love, and doing this for Kenny, who must be very hurt he missed the registration, makes me very proud of you" his Dad said. "If you're sure, why don't you go tell him, he's probably felling pretty low right now" his dad suggested.

"Thanks dad, I will, but do you think we'll have any trouble transferring the registration?" his son asked. "I don't think so because I know Mr. Baker who is in charge. Let me call and ask first", said his father.

After calling Mr. Baker who said it was Ok, Larry ran to Kenny's house to tell him. "What about you?" asked Kenny, "Don't you want to play too?" he continued. Now Larry would like to play also, but it was more important to him that Kenny play because this was his thing. "Oh, you know, basketball is my thing Kenny and baseball is yours. This only seems right to me" Larry stated.

Right then there was a knock at the door and Kenny's Dad answered it. It was Mr. Baskin and he asked Kenny's Dad to call the boys down. "Guess what boys" he began, "Mr. Barker called me back and said because there were so many extra boys who couldn't register, that he was going to open a new team, and both of you could be on it", he told them. "Alright, fantastic, great" said the boys, who could now both play, and on the same team as they had wanted to.

After a minute or two Larry asked, "I wonder if that means Butch Gordon can play also. I didn't tell you but he tried to cut in line in front of me while my Dad was getting coffee. His dad came along and made him go back", Larry told them. "He really wanted to play and I felt bad for him, but fair is fair" he said.

"Kenny, let's run over to his house to make sure he has heard", said Larry. "Ok, but he tried to cut in front of you", Kenny said, "Why do you want to help him", he asked. "Oh I felt sorry for him and just think this would be a nice gesture", Larry said.

When the boys got to Butch's house he came to the door and said in a mean way, "What do you want Larry?" "Butch Mr. Baker told my dad that he was going to open a new team for all of the guys who couldn't register this morning. I knew how much you wanted to play and I thought I'd let you know. Also you and I and Kenny will be on that same team", he told him.

Butch's whole expression changed. "Really, I'm going to get to play, and we're all on the same team" he asked in surprise. "Yeah, but if you haven't heard yet, you may want to have your dad call him to make sure", stated Larry. "Alright", Butch said with excitement.

"Oh Larry, about this morning, I'm sorry I was such a jerk", said Butch. "Aw forget it, we're going to have the best team in the league" expressed Larry, letting Butch off the hook easily. "How about playing some catch?" asked Kenny. "Ok, alright" said the other two boys. "Get your gloves and we'll meet at the vacant lot", said Larry as they ran home to get their stuff. "See you there", shouted Butch after them with a smile on his face.

MANNERS IN THIS STORY

Bad Manners

Butch tried to cut in line

Butch told Larry that he wasn't moving

Butch greeted Larry meanly instead of properly at his house

Good Manners

Larry put his friend Kenny before himself

Larry offered Kenny his place on a team

Larry was considerate of Butch, even though Butch was not of Larry

Butch apologized to Larry for his bad manners

Larry let Butch off the hook easily

Both Boys included Butch in playing catch

STORY 13

BEING POLITE EARNS RESPECT

(Polite—having or showing good manners or respect for other people)

Carly Daniels is a ten year old girl that everyone seemed to like and respect. She was always selected as the leader of her friends, whether it was soccer, or projects in school or just playing in the neighborhood. Her secret of success came from the way she treated people so kindly, and always knowing what to say and do, even in difficult situations.

Carly's parents started early to teach her good manners, and the value of treating people well and caring about the needs of others. She took what they taught her to heart, and it was very evident whereever she went.

The new school year had just started, and Carly's fifth grade class had a new teacher who came in with a beligerant attitude. He acted like he didn't like anyone and was a very poor example for his students.

(Beligerant—inclined to or exhibiting assertiveness, hostility, or combativeness)

When he first walked into the classroom he began by saying loudly, "My name is Mr. Tiller, and I will not tolerate fooling around and not paying attention in this class, do I make myself clear?" he shouted. "Yes Mr. Tiller", came the response from the class as he expected.

Later that day, during recess, he noticed Carly and the way her classmates responded to her. He decided he would watch for a chance to make her an example of his discipline, so all the others would toe the line. He called her to the board and said, "Carly Daniels, divide the number 83 by 23 for us!" "Yes Mr. Tiller", she responded, and quickly wrote the problem on the board, showing her answer, 3.74.

"Does she have the right answer? Quickly; anyone?" No one raised their hand because they were all afraid of him. "Well Carly, the correct answer is", he said while walking to the board, 3.7391" he finished smirkingly.

"Mr. Tiller, we have been taught here to round off to the second decimal place, so that's what I did. If you don't want us to round off I won't", Carly answered very mildly. "You are our teacher so I will be glad to do it any way you ask us", she said in a way to calm the teacher's combativeness.

Mr. Tiller was dumbfounded by her mild, submissive answer. He wanted to make an example of her yet her manner and answer had done just the opposite.

Stumbling for what to say he said, "No, if that's the way you have been taught here, we will continue to round off", he reluctantly replied.

Soon the bell rang, and Mr. Tiller asked Carly to stay behind. She came to his desk as the others left and he asked, "Do you think you are smarter than me Miss Daniels?" still unsure how she turned the tables on him. "No sir", answered Carly, "I merely wanted to point out why I answered the way I did. I meant it when I said I will be glad to do whatever you want us to do in our school work". "Well, Ok", he replied, "I just wanted to be sure that you didn't think you had put one over on me", he stated.

> **MANNERS NOTE**
>
> The whole class could see that their new teacher was trying to stir things up to make an example of Carly. Carly's good manners had taught her that politeness and agreeing with anyone in authority would defuse a rough situation.

"Mr. Tiller, can I say something to you?" Carly asked him. "What is it?" he snapped back. "I don't know if you came from a school which allowed disrespect of teachers that my parents had spoken about, but here you will see we want to learn and look to you as the authority", she said. Mr. Tiller began to realize this school was nothing like the one he had come from, and he said to Carly in a much better manner, "Thank you Carly, I needed to hear that, and I am sorry for coming in expecting the worst again", he continued. "Things will be different starting tomorrow" he said. "Thanks Mr. Tiller, have a good evening", Carly said while leaving.

MANNERS IN THIS STORY

<u>Bad Manners</u>

Mr. Tiller came to his new class belligerent and expecting problems

He shouted at the class and made a threatening remark

Mr. Tiller tried to trick Carly with the answer to the problem he gave her

Mr. Tiller asked a childish question of whether Carly thought she was smarter than he

<u>Good Manners</u>

Carly remained calm and polite when it was obvious that her teacher was trying to get a rise out of her

Carly referred to her teacher as Sir, and politely answered his question, then confirmed that she will gladly do the work the way he wants it

Carly tried to assure Mr. Tiller that the whole class wanted to learn, and knew that he was the authority.

STORY 14

CREDIBILITY COMES FROM THE WAY PEOPLE SEE YOU

(Credibility—the quality or power of inspiring belief)

Roger Lowden was a seventh grader at Hillsdale Middle School. He was one of a group of guys that were in the same class, and also hung out together away from school. Roger had a girlfriend at school named Jenna Smith. The community they lived in had a fair they called the Ox Roast every year in June, and used part of the proceeds to help the school system.

Roger wanted to take Jenna to the Ox Roast, but she wasn't sure her parents would like the idea. One thing that she liked about Roger when she first met him was that he was so polite and mannerly, which many of the other boys in class were not. She asked Roger to come over that evening to meet her parents, hoping his manner would make them agreeable to his taking her to the fair. He agreed, and they set the time for 7:00 that evening after dinner.

Roger arrived at the Smith residence right at 7:00 pm, and wanting to make a good first impression, he had changed his clothes and cleaned up some to meet her parents. Jenna answered the front door and invited Roger in. She led him into the living room where her mother and father were sitting.

"Mom, Dad this is Roger Lowden who I've been telling you about" said Jenna to her parents. They both looked at Roger and said welcomingly, "Hello Roger".

"Good evening Mr. and Mrs. Smith, I hope I am not interrupting anything", Roger began. "Not at all" Mrs. Smith replied, "we were expecting you" she said. "How is your mother doing?" asked Mrs. Smith, "I talk to her at PTA meeting sometimes, but it has been a while since I have gone", she continued. "Very well, thank you for asking Ma'am" answered Roger.

"Well why don't you have a seat dear?" offered Mrs. Smith, "and tell us what you have in mind for the Ox Roast this year", she finished. By this time Jenna's father had put his newspaper aside and was now paying attention. "Well Ma'am, Mr. Smith, I was wanting to take Jenna to the Ox Roast with me this year, and meet up with some of our friends from school there", he answered.

"How do you expect to get you both there?" asked Mr. Smith, "You don't drive do you?" he continued in a joking fashion. "No sir, I don't, but I thought perhaps my father and mother, who are also going, could pick Jenna up and she could ride with us", Roger answered. "I have already asked my parents and they said if that is alright with you, that they would be happy to pick Jenna up" he continued.

Mr. Smith briefly looked at his wife and then said, "well, if your parents are going too, I suppose it would be alright, don't you Mom?" he asked Mrs. Smith. "Oh I think that's fine" she answered. Roger and Jenna looked at each other with excitement, and Roger said "Oh Great, thank you very much, we were hopeful you would agree", he said.

"Well to tell you the truth Roger, I wasn't sure about all of this since you're both only twelve, but I have to say that your manners and respectful way with which you spoke to us tells me we can trust you", Mr. Smith commented. These are signs of good upbringing, and we don't see those in many of the kids today" he continued, and I know Jenna well enough that she would expect that from anyone she would go out with" he concluded. "Thank you again", said Roger, "you won't regret it" he promised.

Jenna and Roger slowly walked out of the room and out of the front door. Once out of eyesight from her parents they hugged and jumped up and down holding hands and excited that they would each be having their first date.

GOOD MANNERS IN THIS STORY

Roger arrived on time as agreed

He changed clothes and cleaned up to make a good impression

Jenna properly introduced Roger to her parents

Jenna's parents greeted Roger welcoming him

Roger properly greeted Jenna's parents, and respectfully said he hoped he was not interrupting them

Mrs. Smith courteously asked about Roger's mother

Roger responded by thanking her for asking

Jenna's parents offered Roger a seat

When Roger responded to Mrs. Smith's question of what he had in mind, he courteously answered, addressing both of her parents

Roger assured the Smith's that he had his parent's approval first

Roger heartily thanked the Smith's for their permission

Mr. Smith politely paid Roger a compliment that his manners were one of the reasons they agreed

Roger properly thanked Mr. Smith for his compliment

STORY 15

SAYING I'M SORRY HELPS CONSIDERABLY

Have you ever been around certain people that either never thinks they are wrong about anything, or if they do, they never apologize for anything? Well Karen Peters was one of those people and she could never bring herself to say she was sorry for anything she may have done wrong.

Karen was an eight year old girl who was very smart in school, and always seemed to win any of the class contests like Spelling Bees, and math games at the board. She also was the one to usually be the first to raise her hand when their third grade teacher would ask the class for answers to things they had been studying.

One of Karen's problems with her classmates was that she was very arrogant.

(Arrogant—having or showing the insulting attitude of people who believe that they are better, smarter, or more important than other people)

As a result of thinking she was smarter and better than her classmates, her attitude didn't include admitting she was wrong or saying she was sorry if she was.

Her two best school friends were girls that would always be telling Karen that she was so smart, and that she was the best at everything. They just liked being around the person they idolized because they thought it gave them status to be her friend (Status—position or rank in relation to other's) Most of the student's in Karen's class respected her intelligence, but were sick of her high and mighty attitude.

One day in the cafeteria Karen, having finished her lunch got up, grabbed her tray, and without looking swung around and hit Joyce Hardy's arm. In doing so her plate came off her tray and slapped up on Joyce's blouse covering it with spaghetti sauce, and instead of saying she was sorry, she said to Joyce, "Watch where you're going" and walked away. Joyce couldn't believe Karen's attitude, and was furious at what she had done to her blouse.

About a week later, their third grade teacher Mrs. Kennedy told the class they would be going on a field trip to the local arboretum.

(Arboretum—a place where trees and plants are grown in order to be studied or seen by the public)

She handed out permission slips for the kids to have their parents sign and bring back. Leslie Hale was a student who was out of school that day, and Mrs. Kennedy asked Karen if she would take it to her, knowing Karen lived just down the street from her. "Sure" answered Karen and took the slip.

Karen put the slip for Leslie in her sweater pocket so she wouldn't forget it. When class ended that day and Karen arrived home, she took her sweater off and hung it in the closet, forgetting about Leslie Hale's permission slip.

Two weeks later was the day before the field trip. Mrs. Kennedy had just checked to make sure that she had all of the permission slips back from the class. "Leslie" she said out loud, "I don't have a permission slip for you". Leslie looked confused and said, "What permission slip?" Mrs. Kennedy said "the one I sent home for you with Karen".

Karen all of a sudden realized she had forgotten to give Leslie the slip the day she was out of school.

What was worse was that she forgot where she had put it. "Karen, didn't you give Leslie the Permission Slip I gave you a couple of weeks ago?"

Now Karen looked confused because she hadn't seen it since it was given to her, and didn't remember where it was. "I guess I didn't, but I haven't seen it or I would have. I don't know what happened to it" she answered her teacher.

"Well Karen, anyone can lose something, but this is important, and Leslie can't go unless we have it signed by her parents." "I just don't know what happened to it Mrs. Kennedy" said Karen. Mrs. Kennedy was shocked at Karen's passing this off so easily, and without even apologizing for it. "Well I'll just have to go to the office to get another form, and then Leslie make sure that you bring it back with you tomorrow" said Mrs. Kennedy shaking her head as she left for the office.

```
┌─────────────────────────────────────────────┐
│             FIELD TRIP PERMISSION           │
│                                             │
│  We are going to _____ on _____   │
│                                      Date    │
│  Promptly leaving at _____              │
│  We will be coming back at _____        │
│  Please remember to pick child up at ____   │
│  Please send the following                  │
│  _____          │
│  _____          │
│                                             │
│  I _____ AND/OR _____     │
│     Parent/Guardian         Parent/Guardian │
│  Give permission for my child _____   │
│                                Child's name │
│  to participate in the above field trip. If an emergency arises while on this field
│  trip, I give permission for my child to have any necessary medical treatment.
│  I release  Step By Step Childcare  from any liability or responsibility
│              provider/center name
│  as long as they act responsibly and are not neglectful.
│  Signature _____   Date _____
│                                              
│  Signature _____   Date _____
│          Form must be signed/returned by: _____
└─────────────────────────────────────────────┘
```

"Thanks a lot" shouted Leslie at Karen as the teacher left the room. "What's your problem?" asked Karen, answering back Leslie's comment. "You know good and well Karen what my problem is. It's your lackadaisical attitude; that's my problem.

(Lackadaisical—non-caring or not important)

I might not have been able to go on the field trip tomorrow if this hadn't been found out today, and you just act like it's no big deal.

Mrs. Kennedy returned with the form and handed it to Leslie. She then turned her attention to Karen and said, "I think you owe Leslie an apology Karen". Karen looked at Mrs. Kennedy and asked, "What for?" Mrs. Kennedy looked surprised at Karen's response and said, "For carelessly losing the form I trusted you to give to her" she answered.

Karen wanted to get this over with very quickly so she half turned to Leslie and said "I'm sorry". Leslie said "Wow that must have hurt. I've never heard you say you're sorry for anything to anybody before this" "Alright now Leslie, that'll be enough" said Mrs. Kennedy.

Karen don't you know that it is good manners to apologize when you've done something wrong or careless?" asked Mrs. Kennedy. "Yes ma'am" said Karen even though she didn't understand that at all. Mrs. Kennedy could see that Karen, even as smart as she is, had never learned the value of saying I'm sorry. She decided she would use this opportunity to teach it.

"Alright, this issue aside, I want to talk about certain things that will be of great value to you as you grow up. One of the most important is exercising good manners, which begins with politeness, including the please and thank you's, and I'm sorry or I apologize" she told them.

"Who can tell me that if someone makes a mistake that hurts someone else, what they should do?" the teacher asked. Karen was not so quick to raise her hand this time because she thought this was all about her, and part of it was. "Ok Tom, tells us what you think" Mrs. Kennedy said calling on Tom Albright as he raised his hand.

"I think you should always apologize and say that you're sorry, so the person realizes you didn't mean to hurt them by the mistake you made" Tom answered. "Saying you're sorry makes a bad situation much better, and can stop the bad feelings before they get started" he explained.

Karen sort of liked Tom so she sat up to hear what he had to say. "Even if you're not wrong but someone thinks you are, it always helps to apologize anyway. I mean, what can it hurt?" added Mary Reiser as the teacher pointed to her for her comments.

"That's very good Mary and very good advice" Mrs. Kennedy told her. "Anyone else?" asked the teacher. Karen raised her hand and was called on. "I'd just like to say that hearing everyone on this subject has made me realize how dumb I can be" she said. "Please, let me apologize to you sincerely Leslie. I now realize that even though I meant no harm, my forgetting about your form was irresponsible of me, and I am sorry for that" she told Leslie.

"Thank you Karen, apology accepted. I know you meant to give me the form, and did nothing intentionally wrong" said Leslie. "Now let's talk about the trip tomorrow" suggested Leslie, and so they did.

> **MANNERS IN THIS STORY**
>
> No matter how smart we are, we are bound to make mistakes. Some mistakes we never mean to do, while others are either purposely done, or carelessly done. When we make any kind of mistake it is just good manners to apologize and say you are sorry.
>
> In this story, Karen thought she was above making mistakes, and didn't acknowledge them when she did. She had never learned to simply say I'm sorry.
>
> After the teacher had pointed out her mistake, and she heard a boy she liked explain what should be done about it, a little light went off in Karen's mind, and she realized it was the mannerly thing to do.

STORY 16

GRACEFULLY ACCEPTING BAD NEWS

Cammy and Gina had been taking dance classes for the last three years since they were eight years old. They had become great friends while taking these weekly classes, and were preparing for their final recital before finishing the Dance School for Girls. All of the girls wanted to try out for the lead dancer in the recital, but only a few of the girls were good enough to be in the running.

Both Cammy and Gina were among the four girls selected to try out for the lead role. Their dance teacher told them that they had one week to prepare for the tryouts, and the girls spent that week working on their dance technique.

The lead role in the recital gave much more attention to that dancer, including time on the stage, and all of the girls had worked hard to improve their skills in the hope they would be chosen for the lead.

The day finally came for the tryouts, and the parents were allowed to come and watch. Each of the four girls in the tryouts took their turn by a random drawing, and were allowed to use their own music and style to exhibit their skills and try to convince their teacher that they were the one for the lead role.

Cammy chose a ballet number as her strengths were in ballet technique. She magically flowed around the stage in a wonderful way that impressed not only her teacher, but the parents as well.

Gina chose to do a more contemporary dance and danced to some current rock music in a very professional way.

(Contemporary—marked by characteristics of the present period)

All of the girls had their turn, and all did very well with the different selections they had made for their time in the tryouts. The teacher told the girls and the assembly of their parents that she would make her decision over the next week, and the person for the lead role would be announced at the beginning of their next session.

Speculation began about who had done a better job, or who had picked a better selection of what to do, and began to build expectations for something that might not be the end result.

(Speculation—ideas or guesses about something that is not known)

Several of the other girls thought that Gina won the tryouts, mostly based on their preference for contemporary dance rather than ballet. They pumped Gina up all week with their opinions that she would be chosen, to the point that Gina began to think she would be also.

Cammy heard about all of the talk about Gina being sure to win, and although she had no idea of what the decision would be, she began to think to herself about being able to congratulate Gina without letting her disappointment show. Cammy decided that whoever wins, she would continue doing what she loved to do; ballet dancing.

That week seemed like a year to the girls waiting to hear who won the lead role for the recital. Everyone was tired of all of the speculation and uncertainty, and wanted the day to come for the decision.

The day finally arrived and the girls and parents sat in the dance studio waiting for the teacher to appear and giver her decision. The door opened and the teacher walked in, knowing everyone was anxious for her decision, so she didn't make them wait any longer.

The lead role for this year's recital goes to Susan Clark the teacher announced. Susan's parents and a few others, including Cammy stood up and applauded for Susan, who was quite surprised.

Gina looked like a bomb had dropped on her, and sat their stunned with her mouth open in surprise, not believing what she just heard. She got up and stormed out of the studio quite angry that she was not chosen, After all, many of the dancers had told her she would win, and there was never any mention of Susan Clark at all.

Cammy

The teacher told the girls and parents that all of the girls had done well that year, and her decision for the lead role was very difficult for her to make. She had Susan come to the front and asked for all to give her a round of applause for winning this year.

Cammy of course was disappointed, but was happy for Susan knowing they all worked hard to try and win. She walked up to Susan and gave her a hug saying, "Congratulations Sue, you deserve it; you were great". Susan said to Cammy, "I am so surprised, I thought you had won hands down Cammy. Thanks for being my friend and I hope we can all go on dancing together in the next school level".

"Of course we will because we all love to dance", replied Cammy. Susan looked and didn't see Gina. She then said to Cammy, "I hope Gina isn't too disappointed, she did a great job also, and I know she thought she was going to win".

"Susan I think she'll come around when she thinks it over. I'm sorry she stormed out, but hopefully she will learn to be more graceful in losses. Let me try and find her, and I'll talk to you later" said Cammy.

Cammy went out of the studio and found Gina sulking in the foyer. She walked up to Gina and said, "Gina, I'm sorry you didn't get the lead this year". Gina looked up at Cammy and said, "I can't believe Clark won the lead. It should have been you or me, and you know it". Cammy looked at Gina and quickly said, "Gina, Sue worked just as hard as we did, and when we lose at something we need to have the good graces not to be a poor loser!"

"Are you defending Miss Wagner's choice of Clark for the lead?" Gina Asked. "You bet I am. Gina, I know you were told by several of the others that they thought you had won, but losing and disappointment does not give you the right to be a poor loser. The best thing you could do right now is to go in and congratulate Sue. She earned it whether you think so or not"," Cammy stated bluntly.

"No way, I won that tryout and I'm not congratulating anyone for Miss Wagner's poor choice. "I thought a minute ago you said you or I should have won. What would you do if I had won?" asked Cammy.

Gina began to think about what Cammy had just said, and realized that she was being a poor loser." Cammy, you're right; I'm acting like a spoiled brat, and have no right to think I should have won any more than you other finalists. I'm sorry!"

"That's more like the Gina, now get in there and congratulate Sue, and we'll go after it again next year in the new dance school we're all going to". "Ok, you're right; thanks for helping me get right about this. I'm going in now", said Gina.

Both girls walked in together, and as they entered the studio, Cammy whispered to Gina, "Now smile!" They both giggled and Gina walked up to Susan and hugged her saying, "Sue, I'm sorry I walked out. Congratulations, you deserve this, and I mean it" said Gina. "Oh thank you so much Gina, that means a lot to me" said Susan.

"Well we still have some real work ahead of us to be ready for the recital, so let's get started tomorrow" said Gina, and they all laughed and shook their heads in agreement.

MORALS IN THIS STORY

Cammy prepared herself if she did not win, while Gina thought she was the sure thing. When Susan Clark was announced the winner unexpectedly, the difference in the manners of Cammy and Gina were apparent.

Cammy showed good manners by standing and applauding, then congratulating Susan.

Gina showed poor manners by being a poor loser and storming out of the room. However, after Cammy pointed out her bad manners, she apologized and congratulated Susan for winning.

LIST OF GOOD MANNERS

Cleanliness—being clean and looking clean in hair, face, hands, and clothes, helps in not giving off offensive odors.

Politeness—Thinking of others before yourself, and being friendly, even when you don't feel like it.

(Politeness Continued)

Greet people politely.

When introduced to someone greet them with saying glad to meet you, or shake hands also if appropriate.

When speaking to adults use the appropriate designation of, Yes Sir or Yes Ma'am; No Sir, No Ma'am.

When speaking to anyone use Please and Thank you.

Don't interrupt while others are speaking; wait your turn.

When someone has done something for you, thank them or tell them that you appreciate what they have done.

In school answer the teacher with Yes or No Mr. or Miss or Mrs. and their last name.

Don't say or be with others that are saying hurtful things in front of the person being hurt.

Be quiet—in church, public performances, and movie theatres, and turn cell phones off.

Apologize—by saying you're sorry if you bump into another or accidently hurt someone.

Gossip or Tale bearing—it is very impolite and bad manners to tell or share bad things about others with other people. Many times gossip involves exaggerations and lies to make the story better. Think how you would feel if it was happening to you.

Golden Rule—Do unto others as you would have them do unto you. Treat others as you would like to be treated.

Excuse Me—say this when you didn't hear what someone said, or when you are trying to get by someone, and also when you sneeze, cough or burp around others.

Do Not Spit—especially in public

Do not cheat at games!

Cover your mouth—when you cough or sneeze, and if possible turn slightly away from others when blowing or cleaning your nose with a handkerchief.

Helping—When seeing someone needs help, if you are able to help them go up and offer by saying, "Here, let me help you", or "May I help you?" If it is the kind of help you can't give, find someone who can, or in an emergency, Call 911.

Clean up—when taking things out to use or play with, put them back. When at a pic-nic throw your trash away.

Thank you for gifts—always thank a person for a gift. If not near you, send a thank you card, or give them a call. If you are the gift giver, say you're welcome when you are thanked.

Don't Run—in pool areas, shopping centers, or other areas where you might run into people.

Taking turns—wait until it is your turn

Sharing—when you have guests or are playing with brothers or sisters, share your things with them.

Opening and holding doors—it is polite to open and hold doors for others, especially for women, someone with arms full of things, or just to be nice to others coming in behind you.

Don't use bad or vulgar language—in public or around others, especially people you don't know.

Do not Bully someone—it is considered cowardly to bully someone, and especially someone weaker or less strong than you.

Knock on the door—before entering a room, and then wait for someone to answer the door.

Be Punctual—always be on time for class or an appointment or a set meeting.

Be Polite to those who serve—make eye contact and turn your phone off when checking out in a store, when ordering from a waitress or waiter, and thank soldiers for serving your country.

Be a Good Sport—Not A Poor Loser

Show the best of social graces when you lose by congratulating the winner

Return things that you have borrowed.

Respect others property.

TABLE MANNERS

Ask your mother, grandmother, or other food preparer if they need help.

Hold their chairs and seat women first.

When seated, place your napkin in your lap.

Wait until everyone is seated to begin.

Never throw food!

Table conversations should be kept only as loud as necessary for the person to hear you that you are speaking to. Never yell.

Don't reach, but always ask for things to be passed with a "Please pass the…", and a thank you when it has been passed to you. Pass things when you are asked. Always pass the plate, platter or container, not an individual thing like bread or rolls.

It is good manners to compliment the food preparer on the good food. Never complain or say the food is bad, even if you don't like it.

If you notice someone may need something, go ahead and ask them like, "May I get some more milk for you?"

Don't interrupt when someone is talking. Wait your turn.

Don't stuff your mouth, or eat and chew with your mouth open.

Don't speak with your mouth full.

Sit up straight at the table.

Don't put your elbows on the table.

No slurping, burping, or humming at the table.

When finished eating, ask to be excused.

Use napkins to wipe your mouth periodically.

CHEATING CAN MAKE YOU A DEAD END KID

BOOK PROVERB
(that gives advice about how people should live)

Those who cheat,
Are stealing from others,
And get false recognition,
Which they think will cover,
Their lack of will to do their work on their own,
And they'll eventually fail for the cheating they've sown.

CHEATING—to take something from (someone) by lying or breaking a rule

STORY 17

NO BIG DEAL, I'LL JUST COPY HERS

Miss Sayer, the new teacher for the sixth grade class at Wilson Heights School was a caring and friendly teacher. She believed in homework every night to help her students get what they needed in addition to her class time. She particularly liked Language Arts and knew that this course was difficult for some students; so much of her homework was regarding this course.

Joel Haines was an eleven year old student in Miss Sayer's class who did not like Language Arts at all. He had trouble understanding the precepts of the course Miss Sayer told the class that they were going to have their quarterly exam on Friday, and suggested everyone study because this was an important test for their overall grade.

(Precept—a command or principle intended especially as a general rule of action)

That week the weather was wonderful with the temperature around seventy-five degrees, and great for playing soccer. After school Joel would meet with his friends to play, but he noticed most of them in his class were leaving early.

Thursday afternoon he finally asked some of his friends why they were leaving early. "To study for the exam tomorrow", Tony Kendal said, "Aren't you studying for it too?" Tony asked. "Naw, I've got it down" Joel responded. "It must be nice" said Jim Walton, "I thought you were having trouble Joel with that course" he added. "Well sometimes I do but I'm getting it now" Joel said. The other boys in his class left but Joel stayed to play some more soccer.

Joel had lied to his friends and his parents about "getting" Language Arts. He really was lost and did not want to admit it for fear his parents would make him study more. Besides, he was sitting next to one of the smartest girls in class, Shawn Quinley, and he knew she liked him, so he planned to just copy her answers.

Miss Sayer began the exam and then announced, "I have to run down to the Principal's office. Just remember you are on your honor to do your own work. I'll be back soon" she said.

Joel could hardly believe his ears that he could copy Shawn's answers, and not have to worry about being seen by the teacher. Shawn whispered answers to Joel so others would not hear, not realizing that she was going to be sorry that she did.

Miss Sayer returned form the Principal's office after most were finished with the exam. She felt that her students would be honorable in her absence, but apologized for being gone so long. Joel was quite happy because he had finished copying Shawn's answers before Miss Sayer returned.

Later in the day Joel went up to Shawn and said, "Thanks Shawn, you were a life saver, I didn't have a clue at most of those questions". "That's alright Joel, but you really need to study because more is coming. I can help you if you like" she offered. "Naw, that's alright, I'll work at it and get it" he replied.

Monday morning began as usual and class was as it always is. At Lunch, Miss Sayer told Joel and Shawn to stay behind while the others went on to the cafeteria.

She looked at her two students sternly and said, "I can't tell you how disappointed I am in both of you. Joel you copied all of Shawns answers on Friday's exam exactly, while I left you on your honor. Shawn, you had to have let him copy your answers for him to have the written answers exactly the same as yours, didn't you?, she asked.

"Yes Ma'am" Shawn answered quickly. "You above all should know better. You both will be getting a "F" for this exam, and Shawn that may drop your "A" two grades for this semester. As for you Joel, this "F" will solidify your "F" for the semester. You ought to be ashamed of yourselves" she added.

Both Shawn and Joel lowered their heads and said "we're sorry Miss Sayer". Joel went on to say how sorry he was to get Shawn involved in this. "Ok, I accept your apology, but Shawn knew what she was doing and now you are both going to pay a price" she said.

"I ought to send you to the Principal, but I'm not going to. I'm going to give you extra work to do that will be done on your own. If it comes in well, I will restore Shawn's grade up one level. If Joel's comes in well, I will change your "F" to a "D" she said. "See me after class for the work I'm going to give you" she added.

Miss Sayer loaded both up with work designed to insure the precepts of Language Arts would be learned. She did this with lot's of repetition in the work, and enough work to use up most of their free time for a two week period.

After class Joel ran up to Shawn and said, "Shawn I'm sorry I got you in trouble". "That's OK Joel, we both made a big mistake" answered Shawn. Joel put his head down ans said, "Yeah, but you were just trying to help me when I was just too darn lazy to do the work myself. I'll never ask that of you again, and thanks for trying to help me".

"If you need help with anything again, just ask me before the test, and I'll be happy to help you" Shawn offered. "Great, I just may ask you for that", Joel said. "Can I walk you home from school today?" Joel asked her. "I'd like that, thank you" replied Shawn. The two became good friends from that day on.

MORAL OF THE STORY

There are many ways to get caught at cheating. Some other students may have turned them in because it is unfair when people do their work, but see others sliding by, copying others.

In this case, Joel and Shawn were caught by an alert teacher seeing the same answers for two students sitting next to each other.

Cheating hurts the cheater because, in this case, Joel was not learning what he needed to know. But it also hurts others like Shawn, as well as others in the class who took the time to study when Joel didn't.

STORY 18

A BIKE RACE WITH TROUBLES

Every summer the little community of Fairhaven had their Town Festival. The annual event had a variety of things to do, including a few rides, a small midway with games, food, and the blue ribbon judging for the best homemade foods.

The big event for the boys was the "Mile and a Half", a dirt track bike race. This race was for the ten to twelve year old boys only, and the winner received a brand new bike. This year the prize was a 24″ Diamondback Octane Mountain Bike that had been available to see on a pedestal at the local Grocery Store for the whole month before the fair.

School had been out for over a month, and all of the kids were preparing for the fair which was now a week away. The boys who were going to race were getting their bikes ready for the big event, and all hoping to win the prize.

(Perishables—likely to spoil if not kept cold)

As the day of the Town Fair arrived, most of the families in Fairhaven had put together their picnic baskets, coolers with drinks and other perishables, and headed out for the town fairgrounds for a day of fun.

The "Mile and a Half" bike race was to begin at 11:00 am, and the twelve boys who were going to participate were getting excited. Most of them went to the same school, Fairhaven Elementary, but four of them went to the local Christian School.

The race was announced, and riders were to bring their bikes to the starting line. The bike course was located on the right side of the park, and over the years had been developed into a series of trails and hills through some of the woods, and also in open areas with turns and straightaway's.

Jerry Pitman was twelve years old and one of the riders. He was not as fast as even some of the ten year olds, and had convinced himself that he couldn't win without some advantage. He had been trying to decide what he could do to get that advantage over the other boys.

> **MORAL DILEMMA**
>
> Jerry didn't feel he had a chance of winning the bike race, and he decided to cheat so he could.

As a result, he had been out on the course several times in the wooded area, and discovered a small, almost hidden path that crossed over from one side of the course to the other, cutting off about a quarter of a mile of the course. This path went in and came out in places that were out of sight of the spectators, and he thought if he played it right he could win the race.

He made his decision the day before the race to use that hidden path to give him an advantage over the other boys. He knew he was cheating, but somehow worked it out in his mind that he had no other way of winning because of his lack of speed.

Jerry knew his deception was a matter of timing. He had to cross over unnoticed and come out before the other boys came around the bend and could see him. He slowed down until the others were out of his sight, then turned and peddled as fast as he could to cross over.

Just as Jerry was about to come out of the woods perfectly, het hit a rock in the trail with the left side of his tire, and fell with the bike at the edge of the course.

Randy Anderson was leading the racers by a tenth of a mile or so, and came around the bend and saw Jerry on the ground with a bleeding knee. He pulled off to help Jerry, and Jerry told him to go on, that he was trying to cheat and got what he deserved.

Randy got off his bike to help the fallen Jerry. The others went on by leaving Randy and Jerry alone. Randy helped Jerry up, and Jerry hung his head and said, "Randy you would have won the race. Why did you stop?" Jerry asked. Randy said, "Jerry, there are a lot of things in life more important than winning a race. I couldn't go on unless I was sure you were all right" he continued, "and cheating, well that's hurts you more than others" he said.

Both boys got on their bikes and headed in to the finish line. Jerry's parents were up front to see if he was all right. A number of people gathered around and Jerry said out loud so all could hear, "Randy lost the race he was easily winning to help me, while I was cheating" he confessed. "I can't tell you all how sorry I am for trying such a foolish thing" he said.

Then Jerry walked to Randy and said, "I thank you so much for what you did, and I am sorry I caused you to lose. Randy, in a very benevolent way said, "Not a problem, but just learn from your mistake that cheating really hurts only you".

(Benevolent—kind and generous)

The next thing that happened surprised Randy very much, and helped in the lesson Jerry had to learn. The Mayor of Fairhaven walked up to Randy with the prize bike and said, "George Dent, who crossed the finish line first told me this bike belonged to you Randy". He told me you were way ahead of him and the others when you stopped to help a fallen friend", he continued, "and I think we all agree".

The people around gave a round of applause to Randy, and he was gleaming with pride for what George and the others were doing. "Thank you so much" he began, this is a wonderful surprise, God Bless you all", he said.

> **MORAL OF THE STORY**
>
> Instead of working and training hard to be able to compete in the race, Jerry decided to use a devious way by cheating. By doing so
>
> (Devious—willing to lie and trick people in order to get what is wanted)
>
> he found out his cheating only hurt him. He surely will face punishment from his parents, and hurt any integrity he had with his friends. Cheating takes something from others, while trying to get something for the cheater that is undeserved.

STORY 19

IT'S ONLY A GAME

Sally Moore was a cheater. She started early by claiming points in card games that she didn't have, just so she could win. As she got a little older, she had become a person who knew how to get away with cheating usually without being caught. She also became very good at getting out of trouble if she was caught. Many of her friends liked her because she had a nice personality, but they became very skeptical of her when it came to playing games.

One day she was playing tennis with Joanie Benton, another eleven year old friend of hers, and Joanie starting to beat Sally. "That was out" shouted Sally to Joanie". "The heck it was, it was in and you know it" Joanie shouted back. Now the ball had hit close to the line, but Sally knew it was in. She refused to give in because she was losing the game and resorted to cheating.

"Joanie, I know it was close, but I can see it better than you, and it hit the line" Sally shouted back. Joanie decided to drop it and continue on. Sally ended up winning the game after several more close calls that were all against Joanie due to Sally cheating.

As time went on, Sally's friends were getting sick and tired of her cheating every time they played any kind of a game with her. Other than games, Sally seemed to be a good friend and was fun to be around, however her cheating at games became an issue in the girls group she hung out with. They began to talk about it when Sally wasn't around, and decided to teach her a lesson in order to put a stop to it.

Joanie had the first suggestion. She would invite Sally to play tennis, and tell her that Mary Beth and Tammy wanted to play also, and suggested they play doubles. During the game, whoever was on Sally's team would tell her that a ball of theirs was out when it wasn't, or in when it wasn't, and give her a little taste of cheating.

"Yes, and everyone has got to go along with it or it won't work, said Mary Beth. Tammy then said, "We won't tell her no matter how much she complains. It will take more than one time to break her" she continued. "We'll later suggest a board game, and when she throws the dice and starts to count, one of us will tell her she counted wrong after the dice have been passed along, while another one of us picks up the dice quickly so she can't prove her number" explained Tammy.

The girls began to laugh at their devious plan to teach their friend a lesson about cheating. "Remember everyone, no giving in to her arguments or it will ruin the whole plan" said Mary Beth.

Friday, on the way home from school Joanie suggested to Sally that they play tennis in the morning, and that Mary Beth and Tammy wanted to play also. "Ok, great" said Sally, "we'll team up tomorrow and play doubles" she said. "Great, see you then" said Joanie as they headed to their own houses.

Saturday morning was the start of a beautiful day, and all four girls met at the tennis courts at ten o'clock. They tossed a coin to see who would be on each team. Mary Beth and Sally were on one side, and Joanie and Tammy on the other.

The game began and Sally returned the serve where the ball landed in the corner of the court, inside the line and was good. "That's out" shouted Tammy, who was playing that corner. "Out, what do you mean out", said Sally, "that was in" she continued. "Sorry Sal, that was out" said Joanie, but pretty close", she continued. "Oh alright" Sally muttered wondering why it looked definitely in to her. "Ok, 15" shouted Joanie as she was serving the second ball.

The game continued on with very few close calls for the girls to "Cheat" Sally with. As the game neared the end, the best thing happened for the girls purpose to teach Sally a lesson. The game needed one more point for Joanie and Tammy to win. Sally threw the ball up to serve, and hit almost a perfect shot landing just before the back line between the two players. "That's out, we win 40-60", yelled Tammy with excitement. "What do you mean out? That was clearly in play" shouted Sally back as she ran to the net. "No Sally that was out, but again, darn close", stated Joanie. "Oh, no way that was out" argued Sally, "I saw that as clear as a bell", she continued.

"Sorry Sal", said Mary Beth her partner, "I hate to have to agree with our opponents, but it looked out to me also", she said. "Oh common" started to say Sally, when she finally realized she couldn't overcome everyone. "Oh alright, congratulations" said Sally to the winners. She wasn't used to losing because of her own cheating tricks, but just had to suck it in for this game. She didn't suspect that she was the victim of cheating, so the girls won the first round.

It was lunch time and Mary Beth suggested the four girls have lunch at her house. They all agreed and headed for Mary Beth's. Mrs. Killian, Mary Beth's mother welcomed them with some sandwich's she had made earlier when Mary Beth had told her she wanted the girls over for lunch.

"Hey guys, let's play some Yahtzee", Mary Beth suggested. "We can play in my room" she continued. Everyone liked the idea, and went into the sunroom while Mary Beth went to get the game. Meanwhile the other two girls positioned themselves where they could be in a place for one to be a blocker, while the other could grab the dice.

The game began and went on for about ten minutes before the first move was made. Sally had the canister with the dice and needed a full house. When she threw the dice, they came up out of order, but she had a full house. "Great, I got my full house" she said as she grabbed for her score sheet to put it down. While she was writing, Tammy quickly grabbed up the dice, while Mary Beth said, "You didn't get a full house". "Sally looked up and said, "What do you mean? They're right there" she said pointing to where the dice used to be. "Oh, I'm sorry, did I pick them up too soon for my turn?" said Mary Beth. Sally asked "didn't you see them?" while she looked up at the other girls. "Well I wasn't paying that much attention, but I didn't see a full house", said Joanie. "Tammy, did you see it?" Sally pleaded. "No, sorry I didn't see it" replied Tammy. "Oh man, I'm sure I had one" said Sally.

Before any more was said, Mary Beth threw the dice and had a small straight. "Small Straight, great I needed that", she told them. The game was nearing the end, and Tammy only needed a Yahtzee to win. Sally had looked down right as Tammy was throwing the dice. "Yahtzee" yelled Tammy with excitement. Sally quickly looked up and saw the dice and there was no Yahtzee there.

"What do you mean, Yahtzee? There's no Yahtzee there" she said as Joanie grabbed the dice. "Yeah, that was a Yahtzee" said Joanie while looking at Sally. "Joanie, what do you mean, there is not a Yahtzee, or was not a Yahtzee before you picked up the dice, and you know it" exclaimed Sally. "What's going on here?" asked Sally with a concerned look on her face.

"Sal, what's going on here, and has been going on all day is our attempt as your friends to let you see what it feels like to lose to cheaters" answered Joanie. "I don't understand" said Sally but rather timidly. "Yes you do Sal" said Joanie. "We have all been friends for years, but we were all getting fed up with your cheating when playing games" she said. "We decided it was about time for you to learn that we were aware of your cheating most of the time, and try to put a stop to it. We thought that was best done by letting it happen to you. How does it feel?" asked Joanie. "Not very good" said Sally.

"Sally we all love you but just wanted your cheating to stop" added Mary Beth. Sally began to ask, "So the tennis calls today…" Tammy cut her off, "Yep, pure cheating" she said, "and not a bad job if I do say so" she added, while the other girls laughed.

"You see Sally, even if it is only a game it's not fair or right to the other players when someone cheats to get ahead. It's just another form of lying and even hurts others at times, when they know someone is cheating but can't or don't want to prove it" Joanie explained.

"I suggest we make a pact", said Tammy, "No more cheating. What's fair is fair and what's right is right", she offered. Sally realizing how she had been, apologized to the other girls, and they all did a group hug.

> **MORAL OF THE STORY**
>
> Cheating may help someone to win, but the winner is really a loser to cheat. It not only hurts people you may care about to cheat, but is nothing more than a lie that lets someone win a false victory.
>
> Keeping within the rules, and using your true self to play can make even losers, winners.
>
> In this story, Sally was fortunate to have such good friends who cared about her, but wanted to teach her a lesson so she could stop the cheating.

STORY 20

GOING FOR THE SCHOOL RECORD

It was approaching the end of the school year for West Side Middle School. Every year the PE teacher, Mr. Hanson, would have a student evaluation for different calisthenics the kids worked out on during their PE classes throughout the year. The school had labeled this day Record Day. Every student, both boys and girls would go for their best record, and were graded according to how many repetitions of each exercise they did in relation to what they had shown during the rest of the year.

In recording these records for each student, the PE teacher also kept track of school records from past years in each exercise, and telling them to the students so they would know what they had to beat to hold a school record.

One of the seventh grade boys, Steve Knight, decided that he was going to go for a school record. He had seen that with all of the students to be evaluated, that Mr. Hanson and his two assistants couldn't possibly watch and count everyone, so each student being evaluated would have their repetitions counted by another student.

Steve began to size up some of the students who he thought could be sort of intimidated into going along with his plan. He went up to Peter Nolan who was a little guy in size and a shy kid in school and said, "Peter, how about being my counter and I'll be yours". Peter was a bit surprised that Steve Knight, one of the popular guys in school, would want him to be his counter.

"Sure, I'll be glad to be your counter", answered Peter. "Great, let me go get the sheets from Mr. Hanson, and we'll get going" Steve said. "Mr. Hanson, Peter and I are going to spot each other, and do our evaluations", said Steve to Mr. Hanson. "Ok Steven" answered Mr. Hanson, "you two guys go over there by Tony, so he can keep an eye on you. First, let me tell you about the school records for seventh grade" he continued. "For sit-ups the school record is 267 sit-ups, and for push-ups the record is 56" he said. "Pull-ups it's 41, and chin-ups it's 55" he finished. "Any questions?" he asked.

Before either boy could say anything, he added, "Remember, your on your honor because we can't watch everybody. That also includes doing the exercises correctly. You got it" he abruptly asked. "Yes sir coach, we have it, thanks", said Steve.

The boys moved to their spot and Steve said to Peter, "Pete you go first with push-ups". Peter got down and began counting as he went while Steve watched with the clipboard. Peter got to eighteen and was about done. He went down to come up into his nineteenth, and couldn't. Steve said, "Ok, twenty five, good job" and wrote it down. Peter got up and said, "Steve, I only had eighteen". "Naw, I counted twenty-five" Steve said, trying to give Peter the idea that they could both fudge a little bit on the repetitions without saying it.

Being a bit confused Peter asked "I couldn't have been seven off in my counting could I" Peter said. "No, you're good at twenty-five" Steve responded hoping Peter would get the idea of padding the numbers for him too.

Steve then took his position for push-ups, and began. When he reached twenty-five, he came up from number twenty-six saying, "Thirty-one", and then thirty-two with the next one while Peter was saying "no that's twenty-seven". Steve ignored him and continued on until he began to slow down. He was actually now at thirty-one but called out to Peter "Forty-two".

That was as far as he could go, so he got up and said to Peter, "so I got to forty-five, that's pretty good". "Not really" said Peter, "you got to thirty-one. I was counting correctly so you must have been confused, but thirty-one is good" continued Peter, trying to keep from a confrontation with Steve, who was obviously trying to cheat.

Steve decided to let this one go without an argument, because he really wanted to beat the school record in sit-ups, and if Peter didn't go along with that, he would then let Peter have it. "Oh, ok thirty-one, what was I thinking" said Steve to Peter, much to Peter's surprise. "Ok then, let's do the sit-ups" said Steve.

Peter got down going first, and Steve held down his feet. Both boys counted out loud. Peter got to sixty-three and began slowing down. He struggled back up with his next one, and Steve called out "seventy-two". That was all Peter could do and when he got up he said to Steve, "that was sixty-four", wanting the record to be correct.

Steve looked at Peter and said, "What's the matter with you? I'm trying to give you an edge, and I might need one in return" he told him. "You understand?" asked Steve trying to intimidate Peter. "Look Steve, you picked the wrong guy if you think you're going to make me do something wrong just because you're bigger than me" Peter responded. "I don't cheat for myself, and I'm sure not going to do it for you" he said.

> **MORAL DILEMMA**
>
> Peter could see that Steve wanted to cheat for a better score, but Peter knew cheating was lying. He also knew that cheating was trying to get a better grade that was not earned. Peter decided he was not going to be a part of this wrongdoing.

Steve realized if he wanted the school record, he needed to do it himself, as he wasn't getting any extra help from Peter. "Look Steve, you just may be able to get that record on your own, and you will feel much better if you do rather than cheating to get it" Peter told him. "Alright, let's get started" said Steve as he got down on the mat. Peter got a hold of his feet to hold them down, and Steve began, with both boys counting.

Steve had been doing sit-ups for some time, and was in good shape. He was moving fast and racking up the "Reps" **(Repetitions— numbers done)** "Two hundred forty" Peter counted. "Hey Coach" Peter yelled at the top of his lungs, "Hurry". "Two hundred fort-three" they continued counting.

The coach and almost everyone else came over quickly to see what was going on. As they circled around the two boys, they all heard, "Two hundred seventy, two hundred seventy- one". Steve was struggling to get more, but finally just stayed down. He was greatly disappointed being so close to the record, and not beating it. "I tried Peter, I" he struggled to say because he was so exhausted.

"Tried what?" asked the coach. "You have just set a new school record. Let's all give a big hand to Steve Knight, now holder of the school record in sit-ups" announced the coach.

"Great job" said Peter. "But I thought the school record was two seventy six" stated Steve. "Nope", said the coach, "that's where you're wrong. It was two hundred sixty-seven, and now it is two hundred and seventy-two held by you Steve", he stated. Everyone applauded again as Steve was helped to his feet by Peter. "Ok, let's get back to it everyone" the coach ordered.

Steve and Peter walked over to get a sip of water together. "Peter, you have taught me a huge lesson today", Steve began. "I should have never thought of cheating or trying to bring you into it" Steve continued. "I realize now that cheating to win could never feel right about holding a school record, it would all be a lie" he said.

Peter looked at him and said, "That's right Steve, and doesn't it feel great to have done it on your own?" "It sure does, and I thank you for refusing to go along with a dumb thing to do" stated Steve. "And now you hold the school record for sit-ups" stated Peter. "Congratulations" he added. "Ok, now on to pull-ups, said Peter, "You want to start with ten?" asked Peter jokingly. "No thanks wise guy, someone taught me today to do things honestly and right" Steve responded. Both boys laughed and walked over to the pull-up bars.

MORAL OF THE STORY

Cheating to win something does different things that many don't realize. First it is lying about doing something you haven't done. Then it is a form of stealing because you are taking something away from someone who earned it. In doing this you are being cheered or recognized by others for an accomplishment that never happened.

Cheating only hurts yourself, and anyone else you can drag into it. You lose integrity because no one trusts a cheater, and in cheating in school you don't have the education you need because you don't do the work.

STORY 21

GREAT IDEA, EVEN IF IT'S NOT MINE

George Washington Middle School announced a project to help student's get familiar with doing something nice for their community. It was not mandatory meaning only those interested would participate in it. The key was for those students to come up with something they thought would help the community, then plan it and do it. The school administrative staff would then pick the best plan and award a fifty dollar prize for it.

Kelly Meachem was in Miss Adler's sixth grade class when the project was announced, and like a number of her fellow student's, she decided not to participate in it. On the other hand some of the kids wanted to do it, and there was some excitement as these students discussed an idea they might have without telling anyone what it was.

Kelly thought and thought trying to come up with something that would help the neighborhood. It then dawned on her. She would take a half a day or more on a Saturday to pick up the trash around the old abandoned strip shopping center on the corner of High Street and East Avenue. This once busy shopping center had been abandoned three years ago, and had become a real eye-sore that everyone talked about but did nothing about it.

Kelly though it would take her five or six hours to pick up the trash and clean up around it, and it would help the neighborhood by making this embarassment cleaner and less detractive.

(Detractive—intended to make a person or thing seem of little importance or value)

Kelly was so excited about her idea that she got with some of her friends during lunch break who were not going to participate, and told them what she was going to do. "Oh Kell, that's a great idea" said Bonnie Devlin her best friend. "Yeah Kell, you're liable to win on that one" chimed in another friend Sue.

The girls began to talk about Kelly's idea and how to go about it, and were overheard by Megan Ansell, who was sitting at the other end of their table. Megan had raised her hand to participate in the school project, but did not have one idea she thought was good enough. When she heard Kelly talking about her idea, she decided to make it her idea instead.

Megan got up from the table quickly and found Miss Adler back in the classroom. She walked in quickly to show her excitement, and said, "Miss Adler, I have a great idea for my project, can I share it with you?" she asked. "Why sure Megan, what do you have in mind?" Miss Adler answered. "Well I was thinking about cleaning up around that old abandoned shopping strip on High Street. That's been such an eye-sore for years and it will make the area look much better" she said.

"Megan, I think that is a very good idea if you want to do it", said Miss Adler. "Just go ahead and turn your idea in tomorrow with the others" she told her. "Miss Adler, what if someone comes up with the same idea as mine?" Megan asked craftily. "Oh, they probably won't, and besides, you've made me aware of the idea early so if they do, it will still go to you" her teacher answered.

The rest of the class came back from lunch and continued out the rest of the school day. When Kelly left school she couldn't wait to get home and tell hermother about her idea for the project.

Kelly's mother was excited with Kelly thinking that her idea was going to make the neighborhood glad someone cleaned that mess up.

The next day in school, all of the kids participating in the project waited patiently to present their idea. Miss Adler was bringing them to the front individually to share their idea. Unfortunately the teacher called Megan up before Kelly, and Megan told her plan.

"I'm going to clean up that trashy old mess at the abandoned market place on High Street" she blurted out, avoiding looking at Kelly. Kelly was crushed and began to tear-up; not thinking anyone would have the same idea as she. She didn't hear anymore as Megan went on telling everyone what a great idea she had, and how she was going to do it.

As Kelly was sad and hanging her head at her desk she heard, "Kelly, want to come up and tell us about your idea?" Miss Adler asked. Kelly tried hard to pull herself together, and then rose from her chair saying, "No Miss Adler, I decided to drop out and not participate in this project". She then took her chair. Miss Adler could tell something was very wrong with Kelley who was always smiling and positive, but decided to wait until after class to ask her.

All of a sudden, to everyone's surprise came a loud voice from the other side of the room. "Oh no you don't Megan Ansell", shouted Kim Stewart, another student who was also not participating in the project. "I saw what you did yesterday you cheater. I watched as you overheard Kelly telling the others about her plan at lunch, and then running off to Miss Adler to let her think this was your idea" she charged.

"I did nothing of the kind Kim. That was an idea I got, and just went back to class early finding Miss Adler, so I thought I would tell her my idea" responded Megan. "Yeah, then why just a few minutes earlier you told me you had no idea of what you were going to do yet?" asked Kim. "Then you saw Kelly telling her idea to her friends and just happened to sit at their table, and all of a sudden a new idea came to you" continued Kim. "Give me a break" she finished.

At this point Kelly was looking up at Megan, finding it hard to believe that she would cheat her out of her idea. Miss Adler walked up to Megan and said, "Is this true Megan?" Megan looked as guilty as she was, and without saying a word ran out of the classroom crying.

Everyone was just stunned, and it was dead quiet in the class. "Ok, let's get back to business", said Miss Adler. "Kelly this will be put down as your idea and thank you for not showing anger toward Megan" she said. "Kim, thank you for clearing this up, but I think you can learn to be a little nicer next time", suggested the teacher. "Yes Miss Adler", Kim responded, and everyone went back to their places.

Miss Adler knew it was up to her to get things right in class, so she went out in the hall and talked to Megan. Minutes later she brought Megan in with her, and was silent while Megan stood in front of the class. She had stopped crying and said, "I want to apologize to Kelly about trying to take her idea. I hope you will forgive me Kelly, and if it's Ok with you, I will help you clean up that mess in trying to make amends for all of this.

Kelly, being a well brought up girl with manners immediately agreed. "That would be great Megan, and would you bring your boom-box so we can play music on your Pandora?" asked Kelly trying to change this embarrassing moment for Megan.

"Sure will, and what time do you want me to be there Saturday? Megan asked. "OK girls, you can talk about all of that later. Right now we're going to work on our math" stated Miss Adler. "Aww" everyone said, and it was back to learning once again.

MORAL OF THE STORY

Trying to cheat someone usually backfires.

In this story, we see Megan trying to cheat Kelly out of her idea, but you never know when someone else is watching or listening.

When a person decides to cheat, they are risking being caught which will always hurt the person cheating, and many times hurt others as well.

Megan was fortunate that Kelly had good manners, and was considerate about Megan's feelings, even though Megan tried to cheat her.

STORY 22

SHE WILL NEVER KNOW

Language Arts class was not one of Fred Wilson's favorite subjects. He particularly didn't like writing projects that were given out several times per year. Needless to say Fred, who was a good student in other courses, always disliked going to Language Arts toward the end of the day.

One day in February during LA class his teacher, Mrs. Kline, called the class to order. "We are going to do our mid-winter writing project" she announced to the groan of several students. Ignoring the groans she continued, "Now I want each of you to write a two thousand word essay on any subject you like. Make sure that your sentence structure, paragraphing, and grammar usage is correct, as you will be graded on your writing skills, not on the subject of your essay.

After class Fred walked home with two of his friends, Bob Shafer and Tom Mills They were talking about basketball and the big game coming up at the High School on Saturday. Fred broke from the basketball discussion and asked his friends, "What are you guys going to write on for your essays?" Tom said, "I don't know, but we've got two weeks before it's due, so why worry about it now?" he asked. All three boys agreed that they had a lot of time before it was due, and went back to their sports discussion.

A week and a half later, Mrs. Kline said in class, "Don't forget you essays are due Friday". Fred looked up in shock. He had forgotten all about the essay and Friday was two days away to have a two thousand word essay on Mrs. Kline's desk. He immediately began to worry about what he was going to do. He didn't even have a topic to write on. He thought I'll bet my friends haven't done theirs yet either.

That afternoon he walked home with his buddy's and asked them, "Have you guys done your essays yet?" "Yeah", said Bob, "I finished mine a week ago. I hate waiting until the last minute" he added. "Got mine done last night" said Tom. "It was a real pain but it's done. How about you?" asked Tom? "No, I haven't even started yet. I forgot all about it until today" he answered. "Man, what are you going to do?" asked Bob, "Mine took me four days to do" he added.

A sense of panic came over Fred. Bob's took four days and he only had less than two. "Well I 'gotta go and get right on it" Fred said as he began to run for home. "See you guys tomorrow" he yelled back.

Fred got home and ran right up to his room. He sat on the edge of his bed very mad at himself for letting this go and then forgetting about it. He thought, what am I going to do, I don't have a clue what to do, and what am I going to do?

All of a sudden an idea came to Fred. The essay could be on anything they liked, so he decided he would do it on science. He had been reading a large book with pictures about the gravitational forces and how it holds us to the earth. That's it, he thought, I'll get started right away.

Fred got his book from the shelf, and opened to the place that told about gravity. He got his note paper out and began to read a little, and then write a little. Pretty soon he realized that he was writing exactly what he was reading. Then a bad thought came to him. Why not just copy the book down on the subject. That would be a fast way to do it and all of the grammar and other stuff would be correct already.

Fred then began to think about his teacher finding out what he had done, and he knew it was wrong because it wasn't his own work. Unfortunately he decided he had no other choice because it was due the day after tomorrow, and there was no way he could do it on his own. He became well aware this was cheating, but felt that he was up against a wall and convinced himself that he had no other choice.

Fred began to copy the book, leaving out a word here or there, or putting in a sentence or two of his own saying the same thing in another way. He worked until dinner, and then went back up to his room to continue. He worked into the night, thinking he was being slick by adding some of his own words or writing a sentence here and there another way. He also thought that there was no way the teacher could catch him because this was not a school book, so how would she know.

Fred spent the next evening the same way, then after dinner working until it was done. His mother checked on him several times and was pleasantly surprised that her son was working so hard at his school work. Little did she know he was really cheating on his assignment and using someone else's writing for his own.

The next day in Language Arts Mrs. Kline said, "Ok, I'm coming around to pick up your essays. Please make sure that your name is on them and also 5th period so I don't mix them up with the other classes" she instructed. As she walked around the room picking up the papers, Bob and Tom whispered loudly to Fred, "Did you get yours done?" Fred smiled and just shook his head that he did, and felt relieved that he had a paper to turn in, but was hoping that Mrs. Kline would not find out what he had done.

Later the next week Mrs. Kline announced that she had finished grading the class's papers. She said that many of them were well done, and some needed work on sentence structure and proper paragraph usage. When she got to Fred, she looked very stern and quietly said, "See me after class".

Fred opened the cover page and saw a bid red "F". He knew he was in big trouble, but couldn't figure out how she could know about what he had done. Bob and Tom both got a "B+" and asked Fred what he got. "Oh ah well, oh never mind" Fred said, stumbling around to try and find some way to answer them without mentioning the grade. Bob and Tom didn't take it any further realizing it must be an embarrassing grade or Fred would have told them.

After class Fred approached Mrs. Kline, who was shaking her head as he came forward. "Fred Wilson I am ashamed of you. Do you think I am so stupid that I can't tell someone else's writing style from your own?" she asked. "No Ma'am" was all Fred could say for the moment. "Then why would you try to offer someone else's work for your own?" she continued. "The only part of that paper that was obviously yours was a few sentences that broke from the writer's style to try and fool me. What do you think I should do about this?" she asked. Fred hung his head in shame and simply said, "I don't know".

"Fred, have you ever heard of the word plagiarism?" she asked him. **(Plagiarize—to steal and pass off (the ideas or words of another) as one's own: use (another's production) without crediting the source)**

"No Ma'am" Fred answered. "Well it is what you have done here" stated Mrs. Kline. "You have plagiarized another person's work and presented it as your own. Plagiarism is stealing and cheating and very, very wrong. Do you understand me?" she asked. "Yes Ma'am" he answered.

Fred wasn't about to offer any defense because he knew he had none. He finally said, "I'm sorry Mrs. Kline. I let things go to the last minute on the paper, and took the easy way out", he said.

"Well I accept your apology but there is a price to pay for cheating. I want you to write another paper, the same length but on another subject of your choice. Whatever grade you get for that paper I will average with the "F" for this paper. That means if you get an "A" on this one you will be doing, your grade for the project will be a "C". Do you understand how this will work?" she asked. "Yes Mrs. Kline, and thank you for another chance" Fred stated.

"You're welcome Fred, but don't ever let this happen again. I know you are a good boy and I hope you learn from this. Never forget that cheating is stealing and lying, and cannot be tolerated in our school or in our society" she said. "Now go and do well on your paper" she instructed. "Thank you Mrs. Kline and I have learned a lesson. It makes me feel terrible when I have done something wrong, and I don't want that feeling anymore."

Fred left the classroom happy that he had another chance, and grateful he had learned a tough lesson. He now had to focus on a topic to write on, and decided to write on the differences between cheating and doing things right. He felt looking into these kinds of things more closely would not only help him with his paper, but seal in his mind the importance of doing things right.

MORAL OF THE STORY

Taking the easy way is very often not the best way and may cause real problems.

In this story, Fred tried to take the easy way out by cheating through plagiarizing, or stealing another's work and presenting it as his own. Sometimes a person may get away with cheating, but not very often.

The lack of respect and trust people put in another is lost if they are caught cheating, because it is the same as stealing and lying. How can people trust you if they know you are a cheater? Think about it.

STORY 23

WHY WOULD SHE DO THAT TO ME

Mrs. Kramer was a widow lady who lived down the street from Linda Goodman, a nine year old girl. Her husband had left her a great deal of money when he died, but she always pretended that she had very little and it was a struggle just to get by and keep what she had.

    Mrs. Kramer had lovely gardens around her house and yard, and she paid neighborhood kids to keep them weeded and watered when necessary, because she was too old to keep them up. As each person who did the work for her would get older and move on, she would find another to do it. In early May she was told by her last girl who kept the gardens for her, that she was not going to be able to do them again this year.

The next day, Linda Goodman was walking past Mrs. Kramer's house going to a friend's house. Mrs. Kramer came out on her front porch and called to Linda, asking her to come to her for a minute. Linda walked up to the porch, and Mrs. Kramer asked her if she would like to take care of her gardens this year. "I'll pay you fifteen dollars per week for keeping the gardens weeded and watered. Would you like to do it?" she asked.

Linda thought for a moment and then asked, "How long does it take to do the work you expect to be done? I only have Saturday and Sunday until school gets out in a few weeks" she said. Mrs. Kramer said, "Oh don't worry about that, it will only take a few hours each week". Linda thought it would be nice to have some of her own money and agreed saying, "Sure Mrs. Kramer, I'll be glad to do it for you. When do I start?" she asked. "How about tomorrow which is Sunday?" she asked. "Ok, I'll be here right after church" Linda said. "Good, I'll see you then", said Mrs. Kramer as she turned to go back into the house. Linda went back home to tell her parents about her new job.

Linda's family got home from church at 11:30. Linda quickly and excitedly ran upstairs to change her clothes and get down to

Mrs. Kramer's. Mrs. Kramer was sitting on her front porch, and came down to meet Linda on her driveway. "Hi there Linda, are you ready to begin?" asked Mrs. Kramer. "Yes ma'am" answered Linda. "Good, well let's start here and I'll show you what needs to be done." she said.

Mrs. Kramer had garden's lining her driveway, all around her house several large flower gardens in the backyard, and lining the garage. As they walked up the driveway Mrs. Kramer pointed out weeds and areas that would take more work than others. The rose bushes needed to be regularly pruned to bring in new roses, and many flower plants like the roses needed to be powered with fungicide periodically.

Linda was in awe at how beautiful Mrs. Kramer's gardens in the backyard were. She had never been in her backyard before, and it was much larger than she had realized. "Weeding is the first thing you need to do. All of these gardens need it as it hasn't been done yet this year. "Ok, where do you want me to start Mrs. Kramer?" Linda asked. "Well why don't you begin in the front yard first where people see things" she answered, "but first let me show you where all of my garden tools are" she continued while walking to the garage.

After Linda saw all of the tools available to her, and where the powders for the plants were, she went out front and got right to work. The soil was dry so the weeds were stubborn to get out without breaking off of their root systems. Linda got her hand cultivator tool and began loosening up the soil. She was working hard for several hours just weeding and had hardly made a dent in the work. Linda began to realize that Mrs. Kramer had not told the truth about how much time it was going to take to keep up the whole yard each week. She also realized both days of her weekends were going to be shot doing all of this gardening.

Linda worked until five o'clock, and put her tools and gloves back in the garage. She had managed to weed and water only the garden around the front porch, and it took nearly five and a half hours. Linda went up and knocked on Mrs. Kramer's front door. "I have to leave now for dinner, and I have only done the front garden around the porch" she said. "It's Ok dear, once the weeds are out of the gardens it will be much easier to keep them up" Mrs. Kramer told her.

Linda walked home thinking she may have gotten in over her head by accepting this job, and it seemed sure to her that she was not getting paid enough for all of the time this was going to take.

At the dinner table she told her parents of the beautiful back yard that Mrs. Kramer had, but that it was so big that there was no way it was only going to take a few hours a week. Her father told her to wait and see how it went for a little while before making that determination, and Linda agreed.

The next Saturday Linda went to Mrs. Kramer's bright and early at eight o'clock. She let Mrs. Kramer know she was there and went to the garage to get her stuff. She worked on another front garden, and found it a little easier to pull the weeds because it had rained the night before and the ground was softened up a bit. Unfortunately, even though it was easier and she was able to move faster, it still took her four hours to finish that one garden.

Linda went home for lunch, and returned for the afternoon. She worked another four hours in the other gardens in the front yard, and managed to finish the front gardens before quitting for the day. She returned her tools to the garage, and came back out front to look over her work. She felt good for finishing the front yard, but was unsure how she was going to do all of the gardens in the back anytime soon.

Linda went to the front door and knocked, and told Mrs. Kramer that she forgot to get her money for last week. Mrs. Kramer apologized and came back to the door with a five dollar bill. She handed it to Linda saying "there you go dear, and I'll see you tomorrow" as she closed the door. Linda just looked at the five dollar bill and turned slowly away.

Walking home she began to think about it and first thought, Ok two weekend days per week at fifteen dollars should be seven fifty a day. Now how did Mrs. Kramer come up with five dollars, especially since I worked five and a half hours? Why that's less than a dollar an hour she thought. She started to make excuses for Mrs. Kramer, first thinking maybe she was short of cash this week, and will make it up to me tomorrow. Linda decided to see what happened when she finished tomorrow.

Linda returned to her job at eleven thirty, after church. She worked on the garden lining the right side of the driveway all the way back to the garage. After five hours, she had finished weeding that garden, and went to put her tools away.

Linda walked up to the front door and knocked. Mrs. Kramer came to the door with a ten dollar bill. She handed it to Linda saying, Thank you dear, I'll see you next week" and closed the door. Linda began to suspect something was wrong. As she walked away she once again began calculating in her head. She was getting confused and waited till she got home to figure it out.

Ok, now I should have been paid fifteen dollars for this week, and probably two fifty more for last week, making it seventeen fifty and all I got was ten. If I figure it by the hour I have been paid a total of fifteen dollars and worked eighteen and a half hours, which comes out to eighty-one cents per hour.

The realization began to hit her. She wanted to give Mrs. Kramer the benefit of the doubt, but this was two weeks in a row she had paid her less than agreed.

Linda had seen Emily Curtain the other day as she was just home from college for the summer. Emily had done some work for Mrs. Kramer, and Linda decided to go and ask Emily about working for Mrs. Kramer.

"Oh Linda, you're not working for that old cheat are you?" Emily asked. Without waiting for an answer, Emily told her that Mrs. Kramer was a big phony who made a habit of seeing what she could get away with by cheating people who did work for her. "She'll act like she is a poor old widow when she is actually quite wealthy" Emily told her. "Linda the best thing you can do is quit now, because she will continue cheating you, and if you take her to task for it, she'll fire you like she did me" Emily explained. Linda's first thought about all of this is why would she do this to me? She then realized she was doing it to everyone. "Thank you Emily, I was wondering about her" said Linda as she turned to go back home.

It suddenly became clear to Linda why she had seen so many different people work such short periods in Mrs. Kramer's yard. They never seemed to stay more than a few weeks at a time she remembered. Well I might as well get this over with now, thought Linda as she walked down the street to Mrs. Kramer's house.

Linda went up to the front door and knocked. Mrs. Kramer opened the door and said, "Well Linda, what can I do for you?" she asked. "Excuse me Mrs. Kramer, but I should have been paid fifteen dollars today for this week, and you only gave me ten" Linda said. Mrs. Kramer got a nasty look on her face and said, "What do you mean fifteen dollars? Why it's taken you two weeks just to do the front yard, and I thought I was being nice in giving you the ten dollars" she blurted out.

"Ok, well I'll let it go then, but I won't be back", Linda told her. "Why you little" began Mrs. Kramer, but Linda wasn't listening. She was walking away with a smile on her face, and glad she had found out about this woman early thanks to Emily. Linda began to wonder who Mrs. Kramer's next victim would be to cheat as if nothing is wrong. She couldn't understand why someone would do this, and realized at nine years old she had much to learn.

MORAL OF THE STORY

Cheating people out of money is a terrible thing to do, and usually will come back to haunt them.

In this story, Mrs. Kramer was cheating, which was also stealing from little Linda who was working hard to do the job she had agreed to. When she discovered that she had been paid less than agreed, her first inclination was to give the cheater the benefit of the doubt, in hopes she would make it up to her.

The next week she was even paid less for more work, and knew something wasn't right. Before jumping to conclusions, she spoke with a former employee, a neighbor named Emily. She confirmed her fear that Mrs. Kramer was cheating her.

STORY 24

THE BETTER ONE SHOULD BE MINE

Aunt Alice's Christmas packages were a huge favorite of the Walters family. She was a very creative woman and had the best wrappings they had ever seen, and usually containing fun gifts. The big box arrived, and as usual, the family opened it right away to put the individual gifts under the tree.

As they opened the big box Mr. Walters began to pull out the gifts one by one, calling out the names on the tags. "Ok, let's see, here's one for Mommy" he called out as he handed it to Mrs. Walters. "And here's one for me" he continued. "Well that's it, no more gifts in here" he said. "Oh Dad, come on, who's next?" Janie, his eleven year old daughter asked. "Oh yeah, you're right, there is some more buried here" her Dad teased. "Now remember, they all go under the tree until Christmas" he instructed them. "Yeah, we know, we know now who's next?" said Jerry, the oldest at twelve.

"Ok, here's one for Amy", he said pulling out a beautiful package for their little five year old. "Thank you Daddy", she said excitedly as she reached for the present. "Oh no, I only see one more" he again teased to get a reaction. "Common Dad, get 'em out" said Jerry who was getting impatient. "Well, see for yourselves" he said continuing the joke, and handing the big box to them.

Both Jerry and Janie dove for the box to see if their Dad was pulling their leg, and sure enough, there were two more gifts in the bottom of the box with their names on them. They each grabbed their present and brought them out of the box.

Now Aunt Alice usually had each present in a wrapped box so they couldn't tell what it was by feeling or shaking. She always wanted them to be a surprise so that they wouldn't know what they were until they were opened.

Later that week, Jerry happened to be home alone and was at that age that let curiosity get the better of him. He decided he was going to peek at his package to see what he was getting, and felt sure he could do it so no one would know the difference.

He sat down with his present and carefully pulled back the tape. He wanted to be sure the wrapping didn't tear, and fortunately, this year Aunt Alice used a foil type paper which made the tape pull back easily. He opened the wrapping and found he was getting an Android Smartphone. He was thrilled and quickly rewrapped the present and put it back under the tree.

Jerry knew that no one was to be home for an hour or more, so he decided to see what his sister Janie was getting. He again carefully opened the present to find that she was getting a Samsung Galaxy Tablet. He was amazed and thought that she was getting a much better present than he was. He carefully wrapped the package back up, and went to put it back under the tree.

As he laid it back next to his, he noticed that both his present and Janie's were wrapped exactly alike, and were in the same size boxes. He began to think about changing the name tags, since they were both the same wrapping, and thereby getting the present he preferred and thought better. He began to justify in his own mind that he was the oldest, and the better present should be his.

As Jerry reached for the presents, he knew switching the name tags would be cheating his sister out of the present that was meant for her. He then told himself that she would never know, and went ahead and changed the name tags. Putting them back, he made sure that everything was back like it was before he started snooping.

Christmas Eve came, and after dinner the family always opened Aunt Alice's presents, as a prelude to family presents opened Christmas morning. Mr. Walters always handed out the gifts, and each would open theirs before the next one was given out. Little Amy was first, and tore open the paper and said excitedly, "an American Girl Doll". She then discovered there were several accessories packaged with it. "Oh I love it" she shouted.

Next their Dad handed to Janie her present. Janie carefully opened the package and said excitedly, "It's a Galaxy Smart Phone! Oh great now I have my own smart phone" she said joyfully. Her Dad looked up at Mrs. Walters rolling his eyes because he knew he would now have to set her up with phone service.

Jerry reached out as his Dad handed him the present with his tag on it. He opened the present slowly and tried to act surprised. "Ok, it's a Samsung Tablet, this is great" he said. Mr. Walters then said, "Great, now we have to get both of you on our cell phone account. Oh well, Merry Christmas" he said, realizing there was no going back now.

Jerry looked over at Janie, and she was very happy with her new phone. On the other hand, Jerry was hurting inside because he had cheated his own sister out of the gift that was meant for her. He wished he hadn't switched the tags because his conscience was bothering him. He wondered what got in to him to cheat his sister out of the gift that she should have received. He became aware of the fact that he would never enjoy the tablet unless he confessed what he had done.

That night he couldn't sleep as he thought about how to tell Janie what he had done, and how that would make him look to the whole family. He thought, Cheating is a stupid thing to do because you are taking from someone something that belongs to them. Even if no one would ever know, your conscience would bother you and make the cheating not worth it. He felt worse and worse as the night went along.

Christmas morning the family gathered together in the living room to open presents. Mr. Walters said to the family, "We're here to open presents, but let's not forget what Christmas really is. It's the day we designate to celebrate the birth of the baby Jesus so long ago" he told them. "Thank you dear" said Mrs. Walters, "we never want to forget that" she said as she looked at her children.

Jerry looked up and said, "I have something I have to say". He then looked at Janie and said "I'm sorry Janie, but I cheated you from the gift you should have gotten from Aunt Alice" he confessed. "What do you mean?" asked Janie. Jerry looked down in shame for a moment then raised his head and said, "You should have received the tablet, and I the phone", he continued. "Both packages were wrapped the same and I switched the tags because I wanted the tablet more than the phone" he told her.

Janie began to say "well how did you" and was cut off as the guilty Jerry said, "I opened the two packages when no one was home, and thought I wanted the tablet more, so I switched the name tags", he confessed. Jerry looked at Janie and said, "Janie I'm so sorry and ashamed that I could do something like that to my own sister" he explained.

Mr. Walters was beginning to say something when Mrs. Walters grabbed his arm to let the two children continue. Janie at first looked surprised and a little hurt, but then looked at Jerry and smiled. "Jerry the truth is that I prefer your present, so let's just let it go and each keep what we have" she said. "I hope you won't try something like this again" she told him. "No way, I've learned my lesson, I couldn't sleep last night because my conscience was bothering me so much" he told her.

Mrs. Walters spoke out and said, "Ok, mistakes were made and forgiven. Let's all learn from this. Now I say Merry Christmas, and let's open some presents". Everyone agreed and Jerry felt greatly relieved, and surprised that he still got the present he wanted.

MORAL OF THE STORY

Greedy desire came over Jerry when he saw the present he really wanted and thought of a wrong way to get it.

Wrongful desires will come upon most people at different times in their lives. The moral person must not give into those desires, simply because they are wrong.

Jerry felt the pain of a conscience that would not let him rest until he had fixed the situation with his sister. Many times these situations do not turn out well or anything close to Jerry's good fortune.

CATCH A WAVE WITH RESPECT & OBEDIENCE

BOOK PROVERB
(that gives advice about how people should live)

Respect and Obedience
go hand in hand,
To show them both, and understand,
Will take you far,
and let others observe,
why you are preferred
by those you serve.

Respect—a feeling or understanding that someone or something is important, serious, etc., and should be treated in an appropriate way

Obedience—the quality or state of being obedient

STORY 25

PLAYING FAVORITES IS NOT THE WAY

Strike three called the umpire as Gil Hanes swung the bat with all his might and failed to connect with the ball. That was the third out for the Badgers, and as Gil walked back to the bench he saw Randy Hill running out to Center Field where he was playing. "Take a break Hanes", Coach Dillard angrily said to Gil, obviously upset with him for not hitting the ball.

"You need to keep your eye on the ball Hanes, and hit the thing once in a while" the coach scoffed at him. "Yes coach" answered Gil with his head down and his feelings hurt.

This was only the second time in the last three games that Coach Dillard had even given Gil a chance to play, and all of the times were only for two or three innings. Gil was used to sitting on the bench with the other four or five boys who were hardly ever given a chance to play Gil knew that he played better than the coach's son who almost always dropped the ball when it came to him, and hadn't got a hit all season. It seemed unfair that the coach always played his son every game for the whole game, while others who were better were left out.

It was worse with the Assistant Coach, Mr. Lerner who wanted his son Bobby to be the star pitcher, but had pitched poorly, and the Badgers had lost their first three games. Bobby was not nearly as good a pitcher as Gil, or even one of the other boys who wanted to pitch.

At the beginning of the season at tryouts for positions, Gil pitched overhand and was fast and accurate for his age. Bobby pitched sidearm and was not as accurate or as fast as Gil. Then came the obvious favoritism scam of Coach Lerner, who told Gil he had to pitch sidearm if he wanted to pitch. Gil tried to tell him he pitched overhand, but Mr. Lerner told him he had to do it side-arm.

Gil took the next pitch and threw it side-arm and nearly hit the batter in the head. The frustrated Gil sounded off at Coach Lerner and said, "Is that the way you want me to pitch?" Coach Lerner decided to take this advantage for his son at the disrespect Gil had shown him. "You're done here, go out and practice with the outfielders" he said sternly.

Gil was crushed because he was a pitcher, and had been a pitcher in his previous year. He regretted showing disrespect to the Coach, but knew he couldn't pitch sidearm, and also knew Mr. Lerner made him do that for his son's sake. Gil headed out to the outfielder practice area, and joined in.

Once everyone came in from practice, Gil overheard Coach Lerner telling Coach Dillard that he had sent Gil to the outfield because he was pitching badly and almost "Beaned" one of the boys. He also told the head coach that Gil had been disrespectful to him, so Coach Dillard decided he would teach Gil a lesson by not playing him much.

Gil went home after the Badgers lost their fourth game, and he felt it was mostly due to the poor pitching of Bobby Lerner. Coach Dillard also had his son Ken at short-stop, and had repeatedly missed balls, some going right through his legs, and he also dropped hit balls that were right to him. It was becoming obvious to the team and to most of the parents that the favoritism being shown to the coach's sons was costing the whole team to lose.

The next game Bobby Lerner couldn't pitch because he had sprained his wrist when he fell off his bike. Coach Dillard asked his assistant who he thought they should play at pitcher. Coach Lerner remembered Gil at their first tryouts, but wasn't going to recommend him because he had disrespected him. He suggested to Coach Dillard that they give Hal Cane a try.

Hal was put in as the starting pitcher for game five, and warmed up. After three innings he had hit two batters with wild pitches, walked four others, and given up three hits. Two of the three hits he gave up were due to Shawn Dillard, the head coach's son missing two ball hit right to him and passed right through his legs and into the outfield.

Jimmy Brewer walked up to the coach while the team was still on the field and asked, "Coach, why don't you try Gil Hanes at pitcher? He's much better than Hal" he said. The Coach thought for a minute and decided Gil had to be better than what they had been doing, so he called time out. "Gil, you're in at pitcher" he said, "get your glove and come with me."

Coach Lerner, who was on the third base sideline, saw what was going on and walked out to the mound. "Ok Hal, time to get a break" said Coach Dillard as Hal handed him the ball and started back to the bench. Coach Dillard handed Gil the ball and told him, "Ok Gil, warm up for a couple of minutes".

Coach Dillard and Coach Lerner walked back to the bench, and while walking Coach Lerner asked Coach Dillard, "are you sure you want to try Hanes?" Coach Dillard looked at Coach Lerner and said, "Yes I do, because I don't think he can do any worse than your son or Hal, do you?" Picking up on his tone of voice Coach Lerner asked, "Well then why don't you try someone else at short-stop? I don't think anyone could do worse than your son has been doing at that positon either" he spouted out. Coach Dillard looked at Coach Lerner and asked, "Ok, who do you suggest?" "John Young" answered Coach Lerner, naming another of the boys they hadn't played much.

"Ok" said Coach Dillard, "Time" he called out to the umpire as the first time-out was about to expire. "Change" he yelled. He looked at Johnny Young on the bench and said, "John, get your glove and take short-stop. Kenny, time for a break" he yelled to his son. Ken Dillard walked off the field with his head down, and Gil yelled at him, "Good job Kenny", trying to make him feel better.

The opposing team had the bases loaded, and two outs. Gill had been throwing his warm up pitches and felt he was ready to go. Gil wound up and threw a fast ball. "Strike one" Yelled the umpire. The catcher gave Gil the signal for a curve ball. Gill shook his head approving, wound up and let it go. The pitch cut the corner and, "Strike two" yelled the umpire.

Gil concentrated on throwing a fastball, wound up and threw. "Crack" was the sound when the batter hit the line drive to Johnny Young ay short-stop.

"Whump" said the ball as it hit the pocket of Johnny's glove, ending the inning.

Both coaches looked at each other and began to realize that the favoritism they had shown to their sons had probably cost this team its losses. The game continued, and the very next at bat, Johnny Young hit a triple off of the wall, and Gil hit him in with a single. The Badgers won their first game that day, and everyone was excited.

As the team finished shaking, or should I say "high-fiving" the hands of their opponents, Coach Lerner walked up to Gil and said, "Gil, I owe you an apology for the way I treated you at tryouts". Gil looked at the Coach and answered, "Well maybe that's what I get for talking so disrespectfully to you. I'm sorry for that" said Gil. "Well I am too, so if it's Ok with you, we'll both let it pass and drive on" said the coach. "Fine with me Coach" answered Gil, and they both joined in to the celebration of their first win of the year.

MORAL OF THE STORY

Showing favoritism is an unfair practice that can cause people to react in a bad way, especially in not respecting those who do it.

Gil spoke disrespectfully to one of his Coaches, and paid a price for it. Although the Coach was wrong to do what he did, disrespect got Gil nowhere. When Gil then remained obedient and took the outfield instead of pitching, even when he felt he was being treated wrong, he remained on the team. He was later able to prove his ability, and receive an apology for the wrong treatment.

Being respectful and obedient will allow a person to get much farther in life, than those who aren't.

STORY 26

A GIRL WHO HAD A BETTER WAY

It was that time of year again when the girls had their meeting and were instructed how to sell and record their sales of cookies. They were instructed how to explain to their customers when the cookies would be available to be picked up or delivered. This group of girls were age's seven to nine, and it was their first year that this age group was able to sell the cookies, so they were told to comply with the rules that were given them.

For safety's sake, they were told not to go alone in their neighborhoods selling the cookies, but to take a parent, or at least pair up with another girl from the group to sell them house to house. They were also instructed never to enter a house unless they knew the person well.

To be able to keep track and not forget what they sold, and to who, they were instructed to keep their order form on a clipboard and have the customer sign for their order. It was also recommended to collect the money all at once when the cookies were delivered.

Elizabeth Tomer was an eight year old in the group, and decided she was going to get started that afternoon, even though her parents were at work. She began going door to door in her neighborhood by herself, trying to get a jump on the others in the group. She didn't have a clipboard so she found an old shopping bag and put her order sheet and pen in it.

Elizabeth was having some success finding several people who gave her orders for cookies. In her excitement, she scribbled them down carelessly on the order pad, and forgot to have the customers sign their orders.

She went down a street behind her neighborhood, and knocked on the door of an older, overgrown house that had not been taken care of very well. The door opened and a big, heavyset man with a dirty T-shirt and unshaven face growled at her, "What do you want?" "Sir would you be interested…" she began, when he cut her off and said loudly, "I don't want nothing, get out of here" and slammed the door in her face.

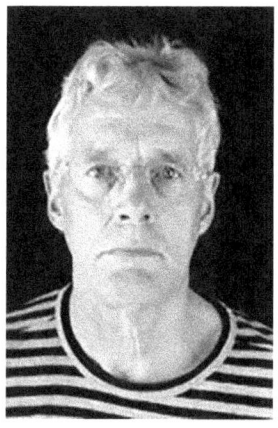

Elizabeth was shaken because she had never experienced anything like this, and she hurried away out of the man's yard and back to her own home. She had been really scared by this man, but decided not to say anything to anyone because they may tell her she broke the rules, and stop her from selling the cookies.

That Saturday their leader, Mrs. Jenkins had arranged for them to sell cookies at the local supermarket. The store manager was glad to help them, but he reminded them about all of the rules for selling at the table outside of the store. "Do not bother the people if they are not interested, and don't shout and yell at people as they approach the store" he said. He also told them that they were not to come into the store to sell the cookies, but only if they had to go to the bathroom, or needed to buy something.

"Thank you Mr. O'Brien, we understand" said Mrs. Jenkins. As he walked back into the store, Mrs. Jenkins asked, "Ok, you all heard him, right?" "Yes Ma'am" most of the girls answered. Elizabeth heard but didn't answer because she had a plan that she thought would get her extra sales.

After about thirty minutes, Elizabeth asked Mrs. Jenkins if she could go to the restroom. She was told she could, and Elizabeth made sure she had her order sheet and pen in her pocket. She entered the store and started up the aisles stopping people and asking them if they wanted to buy the cookies.

Several women gave her an order, but a couple of them looked annoyed that she was bothering them in the store. One man went and found the manager complaining to him about Elizabeth selling cookies in the store. The manager apologized to the man and went looking for Elizabeth. He found her trying to sell to another man in aisle four.

"Just what do you think you're doing young lady" asked an angry Mr. O'Brien. "I, I" was all Elizabeth could say as she was caught red handed.

Mr. O'Brien escorted Elizabeth outside to the place where the group was selling cookies. "Mrs. Jenkins, I'm sorry to tell you I caught this young lady selling to customers in the store, and had some complaints", he said. "If you are going to stay here, she will have to go home", he told her, not wanting to punish the group for what one did.

"Thank you Mr. O'Brien, I' so sorry for the problem but I will take care of it, believe me" Mrs. Jenkins said turning toward Elizabeth with and angry stare. Elizabeth knew she was in trouble now, and waited for the upset Mrs. Jenkins to talk to her. "Elizabeth, I am taking you home to your parents and we are going to deal with this" she told her.

Mrs. Jenkins had her assistant take over at the store and drove Elizabeth to her house. Her parents were home, and once inside they all sat in the living room. Elizabeth's parents were wondering what was wrong, and Mrs. Jenkins began. "I had to bring Elizabeth home this morning because she went directly against the rules I laid out to the girls, telling them that they could not enter the store to approach and sell to store customers" she said. "The store manager caught her selling inside the store when she had told me that she had to go to the bathroom" she continued. "We are fortunate that he didn't make us pick up our table and leave, which would have hurt the other girls" she told them.

"I know that Elizabeth is trying to win the prize for the most cookies sold this year, but this was not the way to do it. It amazed me how well she did on her first day selling when one of you must have gone out with her that day to sell in the neighborhood", she said.

Mr. Tomer said, "I didn't take her out selling, did you Fran?" he asked. "No, I didn't either" responded Mrs. Tomer. "I went out by myself" said Elizabeth. "I wanted to get an early start in my sales, and I was fine, except with that man on Trent Street" she continued. "What man on Trent Street?" asked her father. "I don't know, some old, dirty man who lives on that corner behind us. He was very rude, but otherwise I did fine" she said.

"Fine, Lizzy you could have been hurt or worse. You don't know that man or that neighborhood. What is the matter with you" her father asked worriedly. "Oh he's just an old man who didn't like being bothered" Elizabeth offered.

Mrs. Jenkins interrupted, "Elizabeth, again you are not following the rules, and could have been hurt as a result. Let's thank God you weren't" she said. "I'm sorry Mr. and Mrs. Tomer, but I am suspending Elizabeth for six months from participating in our group. Shen needs to learn respect for authority, and how to obey when told something. If you would, when it's convenient, please bring me her order sheet and any money she has collected, and we'll see where we are in six months".

Elizabeth ran upstairs crying and Mrs. Jenkins was walked out by her parents apologizing for Elizabeth, and assuring her that they would see that she learns this lesson.

Mr. Tomer went upstairs into Elizabeth's room. He had to punish his daughter for her disobedience, but didn't want to hurt her wanting to do well. He sat on the edge of her bed and said, "Lizzy, I want you to learn from this, and understand that you must obey people who are in authority. They are there, just like Mom and I, to help lead you through life so that you are protected and you are fair to others like you" he explained to her. "When you break the rules there are consequences. Now you are out of your group for the next six months, and you are grounded here for the next two weeks" he continued. "By not obeying or respecting what those in authority told you, you could have been hurt or worse being by yourself where you shouldn't have been, and you might have caused all of the girls not to be able to sell the cookies at the supermarket. I want you to stay up here until dinner and think about these things I've said" her Dad told her as he got up to leave her room.

"Daddy, I'm sorry" Elizabeth sobbed, I just wanted to be the best" she explained. "I know Lizzy, but you'll never get there by disrespecting those in authority, or disobeying rules that are set for everyone" her Dad answered. "Now think about it and we'll see you at dinner" he said as he walked out into the hall.

Lizzy laid on her bed and thought about the things she shouldn't have done, and making up her mind to not do them again.

> **MORAL OF THE STORY**
>
> Respect for authority, and obedience to the rules are very important traits for people to have at any age.
>
> People are put in authority to lead, direct, and protect others who are under them, and help them accomplish what they are doing.
>
> Rules and laws are set for the good of everyone, and obeying them keeps people out of trouble, and guides them in what they can and cannot do

STORY 27

THEY'LL NEVER FIND OUT

Old man Wishmeyer was the man who had owned all of the land that was bought by the new house developer. This builder had built fifty or more houses in the subdivision development that the Cook's had purchased their family home in.

Mr. Wishmeyer still owned land with some orchards of apple trees located behind the new homes built on the land he had sold. This was a favorite place for the kids in the neighborhood to meet and play in the fields of the orchards, and of course eat some apples that belonged to Mr. Wishmeyer.

He did not want the kids on his property, and would periodically show up in the orchards with his pitchfork, and hat. He was probably about eighty years old, and wanted the kids to play at home or down the street at the park that was built for them. Whenever he showed up the kids would be scared and run away, and made up all kinds of stories about Old Man Wishmeyer sneaking around.

Jeff Cook was the eleven year old son of the Cook family, and had a younger brother and sister. They had moved into their new house last year, and Jeff quickly made friends with the kids his age in the neighborhood. Jeff's Dad had strictly told him to stay out of the fields of Mr. Wishmeyer, because it was a part of the agreement for people living in this neighborhood.

One Saturday in June, six of the boys were hanging around talking and looking for something to do. George Steiner all of a sudden said, "Hey, let's go over to old man Wishmeyer's orchard and see if we can find some ripe apples to eat". "Yeah, that sounds good" said Sammy Grant", one of the other boys." "I don't know guys" said Jeff, "my Dad told me to stay out of there, and also told me that it was part of the agreement they had to sign as residents of our subdivision" he explained. "Oh common Jeff, what are you a chicken? They'll never know" George said as the other boys headed to the orchard.

The boy's got to the orchard and began looking for some ripe apples. George climbed up one of the trees to reach one near the top. When he reached out, he slipped and fell hitting his chest area on one of the big branches on his way to the ground. He lay on the ground and could hardly breathe. The boys were in a panic not knowing what to do.

> **MORAL DILEMMA**
>
> Jeff wanted to obey his Dad, but didn't want to be known as a chicken among his friends either. He gave in to his friend's pressure, and decided to go with them, hoping George was right that his parents would never know.

About that time Mr. Wishmeyer showed up, and Sammy ran away not wanting to be caught. George looked at Jeff to see if he would run too, but Jeff got down on one knee and told George not to worry, everything would be alright. Mr. Wishmeyer didn't scold the boys as he was too busy trying to see what had happened to George. He pulled out a cell phone and dialed 911.

George was in a lot of pain, and said he couldn't take a deep breath. About 10 minutes later the paramedics, Sammy, and George's Dad showed up. Sammy had felt guilty that he had run, and went to the Steiner's house to tell them George had been hurt. After the paramedics had examined George they carefully lifted him on a stretcher.

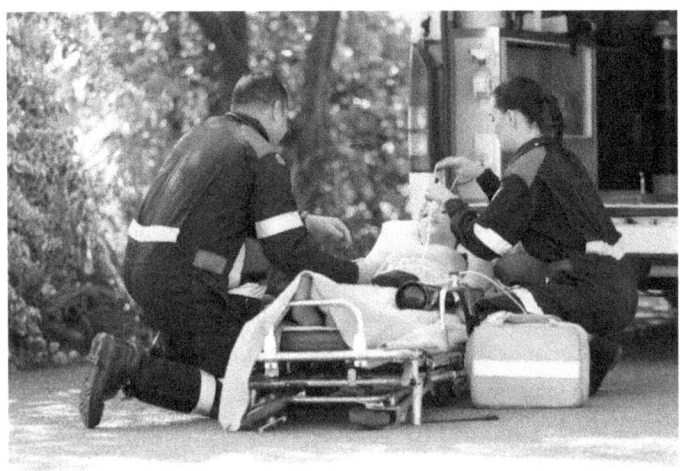

Mr. Wishmeyer went up to the hurting boy and patting him on his arm said, "It'll be ok son, you're going to be fine". They carried him to the ambulance and were loading him in when his Dad asked what they thought. "He'll be ok" one of the paramedics told him. "He may have cracked a rib or two but we won't know until they do X-ray's" he said.

Mr. and Mrs. Steiner got their car and headed to the hospital. Jeff's Dad, Mr. Cook as well as half of the neighborhood had come out to see what was going on. "You see what can happen when you disobey?" asked Mr. Cook to his son. "You were strictly told not to go into Mr. Wishmeyer's orchard and fields, and yet you went" his father scolded. "You all probably thought that we'd never know because usually no one is watching, but now look what's happened" he said." "Go on and get home and I'll deal with you later" he finished.

As Jeff went home wishing he had never given in to going and disobeying his Dad, Mr. Cook was apologizing to Mr. Wishmeyer who had turned out to be a good man when the boys needed help. George was paying a more severe penalty as he had cracked two ribs that would take six weeks to heal.

Sammy's Dad scolded his son also, and told him that disobeying shows a lack of respect for what his Dad had forbidden him to do. He grounded his son and had him write a thousand times that "I will learn to respect and obey".

Jeff and George received similar punishment, and learned a hard lesson which was that thinking "they'll never know" was not true.

MORAL OF THE STORY

Disobedience comes from lack of respect for either the person you are disobeying, or for the thing you are disobeying.

The boys in this story disobeyed their parents because they did not respect the thing they were told not to do, thinking no one would ever know.

STORY 28

COME ON, SHE'S JUST A BABYSITTER

Juan Hernandez and his wife Cara had decided to take a long desired vacation. Their daughter Rosa was now twelve years old, and they had a friend from church who had agreed to come and stay with Rosa while they were gone.

Rosa was also looking forward to her parent's trip because she had some plans of her own that her parents would never agree to. Julia, a friend of Rosa's was having a slumber party for their girlfriends in their walk-out basement, and had invited some of the boys to sneak out and come over after her parent's had gone to bed. Although it was a purely innocent intention, it was not appropriate, and Rosa's parents would be angry if they found out.

Julia's Dad had strictly informed her that there was to be no boys at this slumber party. He told her that for girls of twelve it was inappropriate for that to happen. Julia of course assured her Dad that there would be no boys, knowing that there would be.

Rosa began to waiver about going because she knew her parents would not approve of boys at a slumber party. She got together with Julia, who told her that her parents wouldn't even know, and all she had to do was fool Maria. "Come on, she's just a babysitter, what's the big deal?" asked Julia. "It's not like you're disobeying your parents" she said. Rosa shook her head in agreement.

> **MORAL DILEMMA**
>
> Julia had purposely lied to her Dad which showed disrespect for his authority. Her willingness to completely disobey his conditions for her party not only would hurt her, but her friends also, whose parents would blame her parents for this going on. Julia was extremely selfish in this.

The Hernandez's left Friday evening after their babysitter, Maria Guerra and Rosa had received instructions from them for the four days they would be gone. Rosa had never told her parent's about the slumber party because she didn't want any chance of being told she couldn't go while they were gone.

Maria was a college student who also attended Mr. Hernandez's Sunday school class at church. Shortly after the Hernandez's were gone, Rosa told Maria about the slumber party on Saturday night. Maria was skeptical and unsure whether she should let Rosa go. Rosa suggested that she call Julia's parents to make sure all was fine.

Maria agreed, and after speaking to Mrs. Rios, Julia's mother, she agreed to let Rosa go and be with her friends at the slumber party.

As Saturday night arrived, Maria gave Rosa some last minute instructions about being polite, and not making too much noise that would keep the Rios's awake. "Ok Maria and thanks" said Rosa as she headed down the street to her friend's house.

As each of the girls arrived at Julia's house, the excitement seemed to grow for a night of fun. Once they were all there, and had some snacks while talking up a storm about this and that, someone started a pillow fight.

It got dark about nine o'clock, and periodically Mr. Rios had called downstairs to make sure all was OK. About that time, three of the boys showed up outside.

The boys had figured the way to go to the slumber party without sneaking out from each of their homes, was to have a camp-out in Josh Kedall's back yard. No one would be watching when they left or came back. All of this might have worked if Mr. Rios, hearing boys voices down stairs, hadn't crept down the stairs and caught them all red handed sitting around and talking.

All of the kids looked up in shock as Mr. Rios entered the room. "Ok, you boys leave now" he commanded. With that, the three boys got up saying that they were sorry, and once outside, ran hard back to their tent.

"Julia, I'll deal with you tomorrow" said and angry Mr. Rios. "For now, all of you girls lie down and go to sleep. It's too late to send you home, but this party's over, so for now go to sleep!" he said. Julia knew she was in big trouble, and the girls tried to whisper about the situation, but Mr. Rios was listening at the top of the stairs and yelled down to them, "and no whispering". With that the girls just lied down and went to sleep.

In the morning, Mr. Rios came down and told the girls that he would be calling all of their parent's with what had happened before they would hear it through the grapevine. They all told him that they were sorry for what had happened, and Mr. Rios said, "I don't know which of you or maybe all of you knew what Julia planned, but you need to know this. When you are deceitful, you show disrespect to those you are deceiving, and when you disobey those in authority, there will be a price to pay. I suggest that you who knew don't lie to your parent's about this" he finished.

The girls went home and told their parent's what had happened. When Mr. Rios called, he was pleased to hear they all had told the truth, and had to face whatever their parents thought appropriate for their punishment.

Julia felt bad because she loved her Dad and Mom very much, and never thought that playing kid's tricks was disrespectful to them. Her Dad and Mom had come in to the living room and told her anytime that she was being deceitful or disobedient that she was showing great disrespect for their authority over her as her parents.

"Julia, you are grounded for the next month. That means no playing with your friends, no swimming unless we take the family, and your jobs will be doubled around here. Being deceitful and disobedient will cause serious consequences in life, and also while living at home" her Dad told her.

"Mom and Dad, I really am sorry for letting you down. I do respect you and love you and hope you will forgive me" Julia told them. "Oh, we forgive you" her Dad said, "but now you will pay a price for it, and I don't expect it to happen again" he finished. "It won't" she said. "Ok, well let's start with your getting that mess downstairs you all made last night cleaned up" her mother added, as Julia headed downstairs to clean it up. "And there will be lots of work around here for the next month for you to do, so be prepared" her Dad added.

MORAL OF THE STORY

Disobedience shows disrespect, even when it is done under the false pretense of just being kids.

Julia didn't think a kids prank, like inviting boys over to the slumber party was a big deal. What makes it wrong was being deceitful, knowing her Dad would never allow it. Rosa also did not tell her parent's because she didn't want them to question her, and maybe bring up the boys issue. She thought that by not having them say anything about it, that she was not being deceitful.

When you know the difference about right and wrong, and what your parents expect, it is still deceitful to do a wrong even though they never said anything about it.

STORY 29

THE OCEAN MUST BE RESPECTED

The Boyonton's and the Wilson's were two families where the parent's had been great friends for years. Although they lived close to each other, they were in different neighborhoods but in the same school district. John and Kathy Boyonton had two children, Cara who was ten and Lilly who was eight. The Wilson's, Al and Mary had three kids, Tom who was seventeen, Ann who was twelve, and Gwen who was seven.

Both families had decided to take their summer vacation together this year, and had rented a beach house at the seashore. Tom Wilson wasn't going to go because he had a job and was old enough to stay at home by himself. All of the others were excited about a whole week at the seashore, and had been planning this trip for weeks.

The day came and both families packed up their cars and met at the church parking lot so they could follow each other to the beach, which was about three hours away. After the usual stops for bathroom breaks, they arrived at the rental house and were pleasantly surprised at how nice it was.

It was a two story house with almost a complete glass front facing the ocean and right on the beach. Everyone was excited and left everything in the cars to walk through the house, while the kids ran out on the sand to the water. Mr. Wilson and Mr. Boyonton soon ran out back to make sure the kids were Ok, as they had not yet instructed them about safety in the ocean.

All four children were down at the water's edge letting the waves come up over their bare feet. The Dad's walked down to them, and called the kids to come to them. The waves were making it hard to hear so they all went into the house to set some rules. Mr. Boyonton started by saying, "Ok kids, we're here to have fun, but we need to set some rules down about the water. First, you are not to go swimming in front of this house unless at least one of us is with you", he continued. "You can see down the beach from here that there is a public beach with lifeguards. Still one of us adults needs to be with you even if you go down there. Do you understand?" he asked. "Yes sir" came the answer.

"The reason for rules is for your safety, and you must obey them" said Mr. Wilson. "We don't know yet but the shore in front of the house may have steep drop-offs or even what they call rip-tides that could grab you and take you out into the deep water where you might drown. The public beach is the safe place to swim, and the lifeguards are trained to watch you" he told them.

"Also no one is ever to swim alone anywhere without any exceptions" chimed in Mr. Boyonton sternly. "That is so the other can come get us fast if something should happen" he warned them. "We're not trying to scare you, but even though the ocean is beautiful, it has to be respected because it can be dangerous also. Everybody got it?" he asked. They all shook their heads yes, and went out on the beach until the Mom's made lunch.

Three of the girls made a sandcastle, while Ann just walked along the water edge hoping to find some sea shells. The smell of the fresh salt air off the ocean was very invigorating and the call of the seagulls made the experience just perfect.

After lunch the Dad's walked the girls down to the public beach so they could swim, while the Mom's got to just relax and sit around catching up on things over a cool drink. The weather was perfect and they were sure it was going to be the best vacation ever.

A few days later the girls had noticed that some of the kids in beach houses not too far from theirs were out swimming in front of their houses, and seemed to be fine. They noticed that the swimmers were in up to their shoulders, and weren't having any trouble.

Cara Boyonton said, "Hey if they can do it we can do it!" Ann Wilson, the oldest quickly cut her off and said, "Now you know that your Dad and mine said very clearly not to swim in front of the house without them being out here. What if something happened and there are no lifeguards?" she asked. "Oh Ann, quit being such a worry-wart. Look they're doing it" pointing to the people down way. "Yeah, and they look like adults to me, not kids" retorted Ann.

Cara, who was a good swimmer, walked to the edge of the water and began walking in. Ann, not wanting to be a snitch but afraid that something might happen, sent little Gwen in to get their Dad. Cara was now in about waist high in the water when she slipped from a drop-off she couldn't see. She went under water and surfaced screaming for help.

Ann and Cara's Dads were just coming out to see what was going on when they heard the scream of Cara. They both went running into the water, and Cara's Dad grabbed her from behind and pulled her to safety. Cara was coughing up water and was in shock at how quickly this all happened.

Cara's Dad carried her up on the porch of the house and laid her into one of the reclining sun chairs. Both mothers were there and everyone was hovering over Cara to make sure she was ok.

A little while later, they were all gathered together, and Cara's Dad began a talk to the kids. "Today you have all, and especially Cara, learned a hard lesson in respect and obedience" he began. "We told you not to swim out in front of the house unless one of the adults was with you for this very reason. Cara told me she had seen others doing it down the way, but that did not make it alright for her to do it, and she will be punished for her disobedience" he told them. "Al, do you have something to say?" he asked Mr. Wilson.

"Yes, thanks John" he said. "Respect for the ocean means to understand its hazards as well as its beauty. It is a very powerful body of water that sometimes can drag a swimmer way out into deep water where they drown" he continued. "We don't want you afraid of the ocean, just respect it and don't take chances or disobey rules. Rules are for your safety as you can see from today" he finished.

The rest of the week they all enjoyed their vacation, and had found a number of good size shells along the beach that they kept in bags. Cara was to receive her punishment once they got home because her parents felt she had learned her lesson well about what they had told her, and wanted her to enjoy the rest of their vacation.

> **MORAL OF THE STORY**
>
> Respect for authority and rules is not just for doing what you should, but may keep you in safety and prevent tragic events.
>
> Even though Cara was a good swimmer, she found out that the ocean was much stronger than she was. By disobeying and disrespecting the rules set out by their Dads, and not realizing those rules were for her own protection, she could have had much worse consequences.

STORY 30

THAT'S THE LAST TIME

Robert Sellers was a very spoiled eight year old boy. His parents thought the way to show love was to buy their son just about anything he wanted. He had more toys, more clothes, and just about more of everything than any one of his friends. He was also allowed to do more things, many of which were not at all in his best interest, because his parents were permissive. **(Permissive—giving people a lot of freedom or too much freedom to do what they want to do)** As a result, Robert was not very obedient, and had never learned respect for others or their possessions.

No one knew better than Chris Tanner, Robert's best friend and neighbor, just how spoiled Robert was. Chris had experienced Robert's disrespect for his things many times, and how Robert repeatedly ignored Chris's statements of being careful not to break things. Over time Robert had broken or damaged things of Chris' on numerous occasions, and would smugly tell Chris to just have his parents get another for him.

One time the boys were playing video games over at Robert's house on a new Xbox system that his parents had bought for him. The game was a car race where both competed against the other. When Robert started losing, he became agitated and yanked his control's wire out of the system tearing the wires from their plug. He then grabbed for Chris' control and simply said "Game over".

"Robert, you just broke your new Xbox" Chris said, "What are your parents going to say?" he asked. "Aw they'll just get me another control. I'll tell them this one was defective" Robert answered. "You're going to lie to your parents about this?" asked Chris. "Chris, stop acting like a wimp" Robert said, "besides, they'll never know" he told him.

The next day was Saturday, and Robert and Chris were just hanging around, trying to find something to do. Chris suggested they walk up to the end of the street to the convenience store there and get a Popsicle or something. When they came out of the store, Robert said, "Watch this Chris" and walked by a parked car in the lot. He pulled out his house key and scratched the car's paint all along the side.

"What are you doing Robert? That's a terrible thing to do. That belongs to someone else. What's the matter with you?" he asked. With that Robert began to run laughing at what Chris had said, and Chris realized he had better run also because he may get blamed for it.

When Chris caught up to Robert he said, "Are you crazy? Cars cost a lot of money and that will cost a lot to get fixed. What's the matter with you?" he asked.

"Oh it's no big deal; it's only a little scratch. Things like that happen in parking lots all of the time" Robert told him. "It is a big deal Robert, and it was no little scratch. That was a new car and the owner is going to be very mad about it. He might even call the police" said Chris. "Oh quit worrying about things all of the time. Come on, let's go to my house to have some lunch" Robert suggested. "No thanks, I'm going home for lunch. See you later" said Chris. "Chris come on" said Robert, knowing Chris was mad about the car scratch. Chris walked away repeating, "See you later" and went to his house.

While Chris was eating lunch he saw a police car pull up out in front of Robert's house. He watched from the window to try and see what was going on. After a while the police car came to his house, and the policeman walked up to their front door, ringing the bell.

Chris' Dad answered the door and let the police in. In a minute or two Chris's Dad called Chris to come into the living room and sit down. Chris walked in to the room hoping this was not about the car being scratched by Robert, but was pretty sure it had to be.

"Chris were you up at the corner store this morning with Robert?" his Dad asked. "Yes sir" Chris answered. "Well the police are here wanting to know why you scratched the side of the store manager's new car. It is going to cost him a lot of money to fix it" said his Dad sternly.

"Dad, I didn't scratch that car" Chris said in his defense". "Well then who did?" asked his father. Chris sat silent not wanting to tell on his friend. The police officer then said, "Your friend Robert said you did it with your house key, and that he told you not to do it, but you did it anyway". "He did not" exclaimed Chris not wanting to believe his friend would not only lie about it, but blame him also. "Yes he did, and you could be in a lot of trouble" explained the police officer.

"Well I didn't" said Chris, "I don't even have a house key like Robert does" explained Chris, "You know that Dad, I don't have any keys" he said. "Are you telling us it was Robert who did this?" asked the officer. "Well" Chris started to say realizing it was time to tell the truth. "Yes, it was Robert. We came out of the store after walking up to get a Popsicle. All of a sudden Robert went in his pocket to get his house key and just scratched the whole side of that car. He then just ran and I ran after him. I asked him if he were crazy, and told him that was a new car and would cost a lot to fix. He just laughed at me and called me a worrywart" explained Chris.

The police officer said to Chris and his Dad, "I think we're going to have to walk over to Robert's house and talk about this". They all went over to Robert's house and Robert and his parent's met them at the door. "Come on in" said Robert's father. "John how are you doing?" asked Robert's father of Chris' Dad. "Not too good right now Gary" he responded back to Robert's father, "but we need to get to the bottom of this" he said.

"Why did you tell this policeman that I scratched the car" said Chris angrily. "Oh come on Chris, tell the truth" said Robert. "I am. You know you did it with your house key, and I don't even have any keys, but you told them I did it with my house key" exclaimed Chris. Robert realized he had made a mistake telling the police that Chris used his key. "Well you did it with something in your pocket" said Robert.

Chris put his hands in both of his pockets and pulled the pocket linings out. There was nothing there. Then he said to Robert, "Let's take a look at your house key". Robert was stunned and looked like it. "I don't have a house key" he said. "Yes you do son, now let's see it" said his Dad. Robert reluctantly reached in his pocket and came out with the key. The police officer took it and after one look he said, "maybe you can explain this paint on this key. And by the way, it's the same color as the car paint" he said.

"Ok, I did it. What's the big deal, it's only a little scratch" confessed Robert. "That little scratch will cost several hundred dollars to fix" said the policeman. "If the owner wants to press charges, you could be in big trouble" he told Robert. "Mom, Dad tell him it's Ok, and that you will take care of it" Robert said to his parents.

"Oh, we'll take care of it alright" said Robert's father, beginning with you being grounded without games or TV for two weeks" said his father. "But Dad" Robert began to say being used to getting his own way. "Be quiet" snapped back his Dad. "Things are going to change around here, and you are going to pay us back every penny by working around the house" his father told him. "That's the last time you'll be doing anything unless we know about it" his father finished.

Robert's parents made good on their promise that things would change. It took many punishments to break Robert from his "get away with anything" attitude. He was lucky that the store manager didn't press charges, and he was kept busy for his two weeks of grounding, working to pay off some of the debt that his parents were paying for the car being fixed.

Later, Robert apologized to Chris for blaming him. Chris forgave Robert, and the two are still best friends to this day.

MORAL OF THE STORY

Even spoiled children who have gotten away with so much on many occasions will soon learn that there is a price to pay for disrespect and disobedience.

In this story, Robert found out that disrespecting other people's property, and in this case, damaging it, would cost a lot. Toward the end of the story we're told that it took many punishments to break Robert of his disobedience and his "anything goes" attitude.

It is very important that we all learn to respect the property of others, and be obedient to the rules set down by the authorities in our lives.

STORY 31

OH NO, WHAT AM I GOING TO DO

It was a bright and beautiful September day about two weeks after school started. Kendra Farley was an industrious young nine year old who was always looking for ways to make some money. **(Industrious—working very hard: not lazy)** She knew Christmas was coming up soon, and decided she wanted to make some money to buy the family presents.

Kendra had received a subscription to USA Girls Magazine from her Aunt Ginny on her last birthday, and was looking through the current issue when she saw something very interesting. A greeting card company out of Chicago was offering girls the opportunity to sell cards, stationery, and wrappings for Christmas. The article gave examples of how much the girls kept from what was sold, and the rest was to be sent back to the company.

"This is it" said Kendra out loud in her room, and quickly filled out the form and envelope and mailed it that day. The add said it would take up to ten days to receive the sales package, which contained a catalogue, and some samples of the different cards and packaging she would sell.

About a week later the box was delivered, and when Kendra opened it up it was full of colorful samples for Christmas. There was a little brochure with the instructions of how to fill out the order form, keeping the money and checks in an envelope, and some ideas of what to say to neighbors and friends that she would be selling to.

Kendra read the instructions carefully, and then took the box to show her parents. "What's all this?" asked her Dad. "It's my sample box for selling Christmas Cards and wrapping and stuff" Kendra explained. "Where did you get all of this sweetheart?" asked her mother. "I sent for it from my USA Girls Magazine so I could make some money to buy Christmas presents with" she told them.

"Kendra, I think you should have told us what you wanted to do before doing this" her Dad said. "Who do you plan to sell to?" he asked. "Oh you know, just the neighborhood, and maybe the parents of my friends at school" Kendra replied. "Maybe you could take some samples or the catalogue to work and see if the employees would want some too" she offered. "Well we'll see" he said.

"Do you know how to take care of the money? This is a big responsibility handling people's money, and you want to make sure you don't mess it up" her Dad told her. "I'll be careful Daddy" she said. "Ok, and if you need help make sure you ask for it" her Dad told her. He was a little worried about this venture his daughter was taking on, but also thought it was good for her to learn responsibility.

Kendra started Saturday morning calling on people in her neighborhood. She found that many of her neighbors were very interested in seeing what she had, and she received a number of orders for Christmas Cards with their names to be engraved in them, as well as wrapping and even some personalized stationery. Most paid with a check, but she did end up her first day with about thirty-five dollars in cash. Any cash needing to be sent to the Card Company she would need to get either a money order or have her Dad write a check. Kendra came home feeling very good and showed her parents all of her orders.

Later that afternoon a couple of her friends came over, and after showing them what she was selling, they all decided to walk up to the corner shopping center and have a pizza. Kendra had not calculated how much of the money was hers of what she had sold, but took ten dollars in cash thinking for sure that she had earned that much that day.

The next day being Sunday, Kendra waited until lunchtime to give people time to get back from church. At twelve noon she started out, and sold some of the less expensive items from the catalogue before returning home. She kept all of her samples, order sheets and money together in the sample box on her desk in her room.

Her best friend Helen Yantzi came over and suggested they go up to the arcade to play some games, and see some of their friends who might be there. Kendra quickly grabbed two five dollar bills from her card money and they started on their way. Kendra was making the mistake of not checking what she needed to send to the Card Company to pay for the orders, before taking money out that she thought was hers.

The next few weeks Kendra continued to sell when she could find the time, and continued spending money she thought was hers from all of the sales. One day she decided she better send her first order in to the company. She got her Dads calculator and totaled up the amount she would need to send in. She then got all of her checks and cash together and counted up what she had.

Kendra all of a sudden felt queasy in her stomach. She counted all of the money again, not believing her eyes. Somehow she was twenty-one dollars short and couldn't figure out why. She then remembered all of the cash she had spent over the last few weeks. She had not been keeping track of what she was taking and spending, and she realized that she must have spent much more money than she thought. Now, having no money for the Christmas presents she was selling this stuff for, she was also short of what she needed to send in.

Kendra didn't know what she was going to do and felt ashamed of herself for being so careless, and not respecting the money that was her customers. She knew her Dad had warned her about keeping accurate records of her sales and the money she would need to send in. She realized that she had felt so good about having some spending money on her own, that she neglected to make sure it was hers.

That night at the dinner table her parents could see something was troubling Kendra. "What's the matter honey?" her Mom asked her. With that, Kendra broke down crying. "Hey, Hey, what's this all about?" her Dad asked in sympathy for his daughter.

Kendra tried to calm down and said, "Daddy I have made a terrible mistake. I am short twenty-one dollars for what I have to send to the Card Company for the orders I have" she began. "And it's all due to me carelessly spending money I thought was mine without making sure" she told them.

Mr. Farley thought for a moment about how he should handle this. He then said, "Ok Kendra, I will write a check for the money missing, that you will pay back through work. I know you didn't do this purposely, but you have to realize when you handle property of others, especially money, you have to be very careful. Total respect for people's property is extremely important in life. Obedience to rules that make it clear to calculate what was yours and what is theirs before taking anything is critical" he told her.

Kendra did not get punished by her Dad because it was a careless but honest mistake. She only took money that she thought was hers, but should have calculated first before taking it. Her Dad helped her send in her order and he made up the difference that was missing. He then gave her a list of jobs and projects that she was to do to earn back what he had given her. Kendra learned a hard but good lesson about respect and obedience.

MORAL OF THE STORY

Lack of respect and not obeying the rules is not always done purposely.

In this story, Kendra's lack of experience in selling things and properly handling the money enabled her to do something she should not have, because she didn't know better.

She learned a good lesson, but what if it had been hundreds of dollars from huge sales?

Learning respect early for people's property, in this case money will enable you not to make careless mistakes.

STORY 32

I WISH I HAD LISTENED

Brad Young's scout troop was going on a weekend campout in the woods by the lake. Once the whole Troop got to the camping area, they were going to receive instructions from the Troop Master before breaking up into squads and moving to individual squad campsites.

Mr. Trumball was the Troop Master, and he had Ben Smith sound assembly on his bugle to bring everyone who may have ventured out toward the lake to come into the assembly area. Everyone was excited and had been planning for this weekend campout for a couple of months.

All of the scouts were between ten and twelve, except for the adult leaders, and Mr. Trumball wanted to be sure there was strict obedience to the rules so no one would get lost or hurt. Once they were all together, he told them to sit down and listen up to the rules for the campout.

"Ok guys, isn't it great to be out here in the woods for our campout?" he asked, knowing the answer. "Yes, Yahoo, Alright" were some of the answers coming from the boys. "Now we're all going to have a great time, but this is the time to listen to the rules so nothing happens to anyone" he said.

"Ok, first no one goes anywhere alone except the latrine in the campsite. Always pair up with another scout when you go anywhere outside of the camping area, understand?" he asked. "Yes sir" was the response from the boys wanting to sound like a military unit.

"Even if you are going with another, you are to make sure that your Squad Leader knows where you are going, and that's its ok with him" he stated.

Next, when you hear the bugle call for assembly or mess call, leave what you're doing and come to the assembly area right away" he continued. "Mess call means that the food is ready now, and I don't want any one taking their time to get here, understood?" he asked. "Yes sir" was the response in unison.

"Now there is absolutely no swimming in the lake except at the beach when we will all go down there together. This lake has steep drop-offs in many places, and is safe only at the beach for swimming" he told them.

"I don't want any long hikes except in squad size for safety's sake he said. "And there is to be no fires anywhere but there in the assembly area" he told them while pointing to the open area with benches around the fire pit. We will have this one going the whole time we are here in case someone gets cold or just wants to sit around the fire for a while. Absolutely no fires at the individual campsites. Am I clear?" he asked. "Yes sir" was the loud response from the excited scouts.

"Ok, your squad leaders have a small list of things for you to do, including some of you finishing up some badges" he said. "So have fun, be careful, and lunch will be around noon so that gives you a couple of hours to get your tents up and get settled. Listen for the bugle, and we'll see you then" he finished as all of the boys jumped to their feet with a shout, and headed for their individual campsites.

Brad headed to his campsite with his squad and they worked on getting their tents put up, and their stuff stowed away. After getting settled in, their squad leader Tony Nichols got his squad together to go over the list of things they were to get done.

Ben blew mess call on his bugle and all the boys came running for lunch. Later that night each squad lit a Coleman lantern and hung it on their leaders' tent to enable everyone to be able to spot their campsite after the evening meeting. They then all got their flashlights, which they didn't need yet, and headed down the campsite trails to the assembly area for a grilled chicken and corn on the cob dinner.

The scouts sat around the fire pit with their squads as Mr. Trumball led them in camping songs. Then it was story telling time as it got dark, and Bill Halas started off with a scary story of the missing scout. Two of the other Leader Assistants handed out marshmallows and sticks so those who wanted to could roast some during the time around the campfire.

After the evening gathering, all of the boys followed their squad leaders with their flashlight back to their individual campsites. The lanterns they had left burning on their leader's tent poles made it easier to find their way back in the dark. Once back at their site, the lanterns lit up their campsites so each could get to their tents and ready themselves for the night's sleep.

The scouts went to sleep talking with their tent mates about what fun they were having, and wondering what the next day would bring. It seemed like they had just fallen off to sleep when the sound of Reveille broke the early morning air from the assembly area. "Ok everybody, let's get up and hit the latrine and wash up for breakfast" shouted the squad leader. "Come on, come on" he said, "we need to be up, dressed and ready for mess call" he told the yawning boys just beginning to stir in their sleeping bags.

Although it was summer, getting out of a warm sleeping bag at six-thirty in the morning brought a chill to the boys, and they hurried to get dressed. After all had washed up and brushed their teeth, they quickly went back to their tents and rolled up sleeping bags and straightened up the inside of their tents in case there would be an inspection.

At seven o'clock sharp, they heard the bugler blow out mess call, meaning it was time for breakfast. "I could eat a horse" said Brad as they all began to walk quickly down the trail to the assembly area. "Me too" chimed in Jimmy Alt.

After breakfast, two of the boys were picked for KP duty, to wash the breakfast dishes, while the others walked back to their tents to prepare for the day. Brad and Jimmy had been chosen, and they took it in good measure, staying back at the assemble area to wash the dishes. They talked while they cleaned up, and after they were through Mr. Trumball sent them back to their campsite to check in with their squad leader.

Surprisingly, when they got to the campsite, it was empty. "What do we do?" asked Jimmy, as they had no idea where their squad had gone. "I don't know" Brad replied, "But they are probably out hiking" he offered. "Come on, let's see if we can catch up" Brad said, starting down the trail in a direction they had never gone. "Wait Brad" said Jimmy, "we better check in with Mr. Trumball to see what we should do" he told him.

"Naw, it's ok" said Brad, "We are paired up as they told us, and I'll bet they just followed this trail" he explained. A nervous Jimmy told him ok and off they went down the trail that Brad seemed he was sure they took.

After walking about thirty minutes, Jimmy finally spoke up and said "Brad, I don't think this is the way they went". Brad by this time was no so sure himself anymore. He saw another trail to the right and suggested that they try this one. "All of these trails have to end up back at camp" he told Jimmy hoping he was right. "This one looks like it is swinging around back in the direction we came" he offered, so let's see if it takes us back.

Well the second trail did not take them back, in fact it started to wind around so much that the two boys had no idea which direction was back anymore. They began to realize that they were lost, and stopped to try and decide what to do next. "Should we just stay here and hope someone comes for us?" asked Jimmy, "or do we try and go back another way?" he asked.

Brad, not feeling so bold anymore just sort of slumped his shoulders and said, "I don't know what to do. Let's just sit down and teak a break" he said. Both boys sat down on the ground and began to imagine the worse things that could happen. "What if it gets dark? Then what do we do?" asked a scared Jimmy. "We'll we still have plenty of daylight left" offered Brad, not wanting to think about Jimmy's question.

The two lost boys just sat in place for about an hour. Periodically one would say, "Did you hear that?" in hopes the other had heard someone yelling their name out. "Naw, it's just the wind" the other would say. They finally rose to their feet deciding that they had to do something, but weren't sure what that was.

"Ok, walking is better than sitting, and hopefully we'll see or hear something" offered Brad to Jimmy. Just as they began to walk, Jimmy stopped and said, "Brad I heard something!" "Knock it off Jimmy and let's get going" Brad said. Then Brad stopped and said, "Yes, I did hear something, let's listen" he told Jimmy.

Both boys sort of stretched their necks up turning this way and that, trying to see if they really did hear something. All of a sudden Brad yelled out, "We're here, we're here" as loud as he could. Then they both heard Mr. Trumball's deep voice saying, "Where, where are you?" "Over here, over here" both boys yelled repeatedly. Then they saw him, along with another of their squad guys running to meet them. It turns out their whole squad was looking for them. They were so glad that they had been found, and their ordeal was over.

Every one walked back through the woods for about thirty minutes and finally arrived at the assembly area. Mr. Trumball had called ahead to let everyone else know that the boys were safe and sound.

Everyone had missed their lunch looking for the two lost boys, so once back, Mr. Trumball suggested that they have an early dinner and discuss the day's events.

Once everyone had eaten, Mr. Trumball had them all sit down and began the discussion. "Ok, today we had a lesson in why it's important to obey all of the rules, not just some of them" he began. "Brad and Jimmy obeyed one of the rules about not going outside the campsite unless being paired up. The rule they didn't follow was to let the leader know where they were going. Since their squad leader was not to be found to tell that to, they should have come back to the assembly area to tell me or one of the other leaders" he told them. "As a result, they got very lost which caused them both a lot of stress and uncertainty. Right Boys?" he asked them. Jimmy and Brad sort of hung their heads responding a soft, "Yes sir".

"Fortunately, we found them before it got dark or we might have had a real problem" he told them. "Now, I'm going to ask you all, and I want all of you to respond. Which rules do we obey?" he asked. "All of them" came the yell from all of the boys. "And if we aren't sure about the rules, who do we ask?" he asked. "Our leaders" came the response. "Very good, now let's enjoy the rest of the day just relaxing" he told them. With that, all of the boys went back to their campsites and just hung out.

> **MORAL OF THE STORY**
>
> Following just some of the rules is not enough. They are all made to direct people and keep them safe.
>
> In this story, Brad and Jimmy thought they'd be alright trying to locate the rest of their squad on their own, but got hopelessly lost. If they had asked Mr. Trumball, he would have told them that their squad had gone another way, and to wait for them because they'd be back soon.
>
> Fortunately, everything turned out alright, but what if it had gotten dark? Then what?

ABOUT THE AUTHOR

Richard L. McBain is the father of two adult sons, and a husband of forty-three years. He worked as a youth counselor for teenage wards of a county in Ohio, and later as a director of three corporations.

He has held the positions of Chief Operating Officer, General Manager, and/or Vice President of six different companies. He now serves as President and CEO Triune Group, Inc. in Marietta, Georgia.

Dick McBain, 66, has been a Christian all of his life and a student of the Bible for the last 38 years. He has authored and published four other books, and wanted to help children learn about morals and manners in a fun way through short stories that would interest them. He has four grand-children and believes the kids today need some help learning these important principles.

www.ingramcontent.com/pod-product-compliance
Lightning Source LLC
LaVergne TN
LVHW011933070526
838202LV00054B/4621